ASSASSINS!

STANTON
For him killing was more than a science—it was an art. Few knew his name; fewer still, his reputation. Those few wanted a President killed!

KARL
An ex-Nazi soldier with a tortured conscience, he was out to expiate the sins of his past.

BARBRA
As a girl she had been kidnapped by the Nazis. As a woman she was an expert on aviation, and the erotic way to the heart of Amin's personal pilot.

LAJEBA
The only Black Ugandan in the group, he saw the effects of Amin's barbarism and risked all to save his nation from savagery.

WEAVER
The Australian with a glass eye had once killed the wrong man with his bare hands—this time there would be no mistake.

CARTER
He'd had so many women he'd lost count. He would work for or against the law, depending on who paid most.

The Killing of IDI AMIN

LESLIE WATKINS

AVON
PUBLISHERS OF BARD, CAMELOT AND DISCUS BOOKS

AVON BOOKS
A division of
The Hearst Corporation
959 Eighth Avenue
New York, New York 10019

First Avon Printing, June, 1977

Printed in Canada

To Simon

PREFACE

Sunday, September 17, 1972, looked like being a quiet day in Fleet Street. I telephoned my wife from the newsroom of the *Daily Mail* to say I would be home early. Twenty minutes later Louis Kirby, then Deputy Editor of the paper, told me he had other plans for my evening.

Confused reports were filtering through about an attempted invasion of Uganda by forces from Tanzania. I was to go to the battle zone and would be travelling on the night flight from Gatwick.

Our aircraft reached Entebbe in the early dawn. The aircrew was due to be relieved there, with a new team flying the plane on to its final destination in Nairobi. However, the situation in Uganda was then so volatile—and Amin's men were reported as being so aggressively "trigger-happy"—that the captain refused to allow his crew to disembark. Rooms had been booked for them at an hotel near the airport but he felt it was not safe for them to leave the aircraft. They were therefore to stay on board as passengers for the last leg of the flight to Kenya.

Not one of the other passengers was leaving the aircraft at Entebbe either. So I crossed the tarmac on my own and passed under the huge sign which—sardonically, some might feel—said: "Welcome to Uganda."

I had already travelled extensively, mainly on newspaper assignments, but it was my first visit to this part of Africa.

As I waited for my entry visa—which was given with surprising speed and lack of formality—I passed a queue of tired and bedraggled Asians who were in the process of being deported to Britain. These were people who were later to complain, almost certainly with justification, that their few remaining items of value—such as watches and wedding rings—were forcibly stolen from them by the military rabble at the airport.

About seven hours later I was arrested at gun-point and thrown into prison in Kampala. My "crime" seemed to be that I had a white face and a British passport which, of course, was seized by my captors.

The sessions of interrogation which followed, some almost apologetically gentle and some violently hostile, made it clear that I was suspected of being a spy.

Eventually I was escorted back to Entebbe and deported as an "undesirable immigrant."

So I saw far more of the inside of that dungeon than I did of the sights of Uganda. However, my captivity did provide me with an unusual insight into the horrors which were being perpetrated in that beautiful land, for I was wedged-in—sleeping rough on the filthy concrete—with a strange mix of men and women from a range of backgrounds. There were Asians, black Africans, whites from many parts of the world and a group of terrified young hippies from Tanzania who, having been captured while on a hitch-hike holiday, were facing the prospect of almost-certain death.

Some, possibly, had committed major crimes. Others had committed minor crimes. The majority, as far as one could assess, had committed no crimes.

We talked. We talked about our experiences and about the barbaric regime of terror which was supreme in Uganda. And from my companions in fear I learned a great deal.

My feelings towards the people of Uganda have in no way been darkened by my experiences in that prison. The majority of those I have met, inside Uganda and in other countries, are pleasant and warm-hearted. Even some of the prison guards, at no small risk to themselves, occasionally demonstrated those qualities—being obviously embarrassed by the duties they were obliged to perform. These people were helpless against the evil which had taken grip of their land.

This book, of course, is fiction. I cannot claim, for instance, to have knowledge of private conversations which may have taken place within the security of Amin's home. Most of the men and women who people the following pages are also fictitious. But, having said that, I must stress one point which I am sure will become obvious to most readers: this novel is built on a foundation of obscenely-horrific facts.

The atrocities committed under the Amin regime—together with the savage and often preposterous outbursts of this egocentric dictator—are well-documented.

Many attempts have been made on Amin's life. It would be surprising, in view of the desperation and the bitterness of his countless enemies, if there were not more. However, I have no personal knowledge of any assassination plots—past, present or future. And this novel in no way implies that I would endorse or applaud any such plot.

I am merely using the nightmare realities as a springboard for what is a high dive into the realms of imagination. This, as I have said, is fiction. Many expert commentators are convinced, however, that some variation of it will one day become fact.

Leslie Watkins
March, 1976

CHAPTER 1

At twenty minutes past three in the afternoon the haggard man knew he was about to die. That was when he saw the guard coming across the dusty yard of the prison with the iron-headed mallet. That, he knew, was the instrument of execution. And yet he felt curiously and floatingly detached. It was unreal, as if he was standing outside himself and was merely watching the bizarre scene being unfolded in a film.

All of it was unreal. It had been unreal since that first moment when they had seized him . . .

He had been fishing then at Lake Nakivali, near his home village of Kahirimbi, and the day had been good. With the sun nearly setting, he had strapped the basket of catfish to his bicycle. They were fine fish, fish which would get a good price in Mbarara. And the money was needed more than ever for there was this extra mouth. His wife had just given him his first child . . .

Their truck had been pulled across the narrow dirt road and they had stopped him. The bicycle, they had told him, was too *malidadi*—too new and smart—to belong to a scavenger of fish. He must have stolen it. They had to do their duty as soldiers. They had to confiscate stolen property.

He had argued and protested and then, losing his temper, he had cursed at them. Then the officer—who would perhaps merely have taken the bicycle and left him to go home in peace—had also become angry.

The officer had shouted that such wickedness would surely bring forth the wrath of Edeke.

Edeke. He was one of the dreaded gods—the god who fathered all calamities. Venereal disease and rinderpest . . . pain and sudden death . . . these were the gifts of Edeke.

As they had dragged away his bicycle they had told him he would be charged with theft. He would be taken to a courthouse and he would be tried.

Then they had tied his hands and driven him through the darkness. On the distant hills there had been the familiar splashes of orange—fires tended by herdsmen to protect their cattle from the lions.

There had been no one and nothing to protect him. And he had known then that there would be no trial.

And now it was twenty minutes past three in the afternoon. And the man was coming with the mallet. And he knew he was going to die.

The two soldiers grabbed him and started to drag him towards the middle of the yard where the concrete was stained with the blood of yesterday.

And suddenly it was real. A cold ball of fear in his stomach exploded through his whole body and his skinny limbs started to twitch in pathetic spasms of resistance. But he was weak, weak because of the days of hunger and torture, and the men grinned as they forced him on to his back and pinned him to the ground.

For a brief instance he glimpsed the blueness of the sky. The tranquil and almost welcoming blueness of eternity. Then the head of that terrible mallet was arcing down towards his face.

His death-scream was still lingering in the still air when the flies started swarming hungrily in his blood and his pulped brain.

And in a quiet corner the observer looked on. He showed no emotion, but just watched. And later, much later, he made a brief note of the incident. The note eventually went into the Blue Dossier which was being maintained so meticulously in Chicago, Illinois.

*   *   *

There were no proper windows in the banqueting room —just a huge dome of frosted glass directly over the round wooden table. The walls, decorated with shields and ceremonial spears, were panelled with fumed oak. The air was stifling with incense and the smell of stale sweat. It was an oppressive room and a claustrophobic one.

But now it was alive with conversation and laughter, for this was a special evening of celebration. January 25, the anniversary of Idi Amin's take-over in Uganda.

And there in the room, near the heart of the Presidential Palace in Kampala, was Amin with seven of his senior aides—men who had helped topple Milton Obote from power—starting their feast of self-congratulation.

Moloro, the President's chief bodyguard, was at attention near the door. And as he watched his master he pondered on the stupidity of foreigners. There were so many people in so many countries who had made the mistake of seeing the General as a figure of fun.

To the fools of the world he was little more than a buffoon who, because of some quirk of fate, was able to play-act at being an international politician.

Moloro knew better. He knew that no man could seize and hold control of such a volatile country without shrewdness and a deviously-sophisticated judgment. They were fine qualities, qualities to be admired.

Moloro was proud that his own ancestry should have run so parallel to that of this great man. Both were from sound Nubian stock. And from their parents they had inherited similar magnificent physiques—the sort of physique which had helped the President become the heavyweight boxing champion of Uganda. They had also inherited the old superstitions and the old capacity for sadism.

There were others who saw it from a more detached view-point . . .

The vibrant blood of Africa . . . pulsing down through the generations . . . sweeping the ancient beliefs and barbarisms into the twentieth century. So many of the obscene cruelties of the seventies had once been fermenting in the sperm of men long dead. They were lingering on, those old fears and convictions. Human sacrifices continued to be made to appease the unseen ones swarming through the jungle undergrowth and whispering balefully across the deserts of darkness . . .

Occasionally, at that banqueting table, Amin would release high-pitched giggles of glee, rather like a self-consciously naughty schoolboy, and his guests laughed obediently. They knew his unpredictability. They had often seen how light-heartedness could vanish in a sudden outburst of insane rage.

He was bantering with them now, regaling them with ribald jokes, but still he exuded an aura of brooding menace. They were starting their soup when he suddenly rose to his feet and raised his glass high.

"My friends!" He beamed at them, his eyes lingering with apparent affection on one face after another. They were all standing instantly, glasses in their hands.

"My friends! We will drink in salutation to the Muzimu!"

"The Muzimu!" they echoed enthusiastically.

This was a special toast, a sacred toast. For as Amin had explained to them many times, the regime was secure in the all-embracing protection of the Muzimu. The spirits of the dead. It was they who had guided Amin as he had plotted to take control of Uganda. It was the Muzimu who, with the wisdom of forever, had counselled him through his years of rule and had often saved him from his enemies.

There had been occasions when he had talked with the dead, had chatted informally with them about the events of the following day or the following year. And it was the dead who had given him the details of how and when his own life would end. He had told the entire nation about that in a broadcast, but had explained: "I am not prepared to reveal the date of my death because that is a State secret—one which, if it were to be released, would be used by the enemies of Uganda."

So they drank to the Muzimu. Then, following Amin's lead, they again sat down to their soup. But Amin did not pick up his spoon.

"You know—all of you know—that I am the favoured son of the Muzimu," he said.

It was a categoric statement of fact. They nodded cautiously and mumbled their agreement but, knowing his tendency to leap at dangerous tangents, they were wondering why he should be telling them what they all knew so well.

Moloro alone was not wondering. Moloro already knew.

"Good!" said Amin. He smiled with favour at them, obviously pleased with their reaction. "Their favourite son! Yet how many times have the misguided ones tried to pit their pathetic strength, in defiance of the Muzimu, against the destiny of Uganda? How many times have they tried to change the unchangeable course of history by killing me before my death date? You, Kagwa—how many times?"

Kagwa was an old man. He was a colonel, not so much because of his ability but because, like Amin, he had tribal ties with the people of southern Sudan. His family was trusted. Now he was apprehensive about this special attention and his lower lip twitched involuntarily. "Many times, I regret, Mr. President," he said tentatively. "There have been too many bad men."

Amin nodded. "Yes, many times. And every time the misguided ones have joined the Muzimu. They have joined them, not just as a punishment but so that they can share the wisdom of the Muzimu. They have gone to be taught how wrong they were—how they were offending against Uganda—so that they can become part of the great shield that surrounds me. My enemies are killed so that they can join the ranks of my protectors!"

"Praise to the Muzimu," murmured the man on his left. "Honour to the Muzimu."

Amin ignored him. "I have not spoken of it before but there have been more misguided ones. Yesterday another attempt was made to kill me. It was stopped because of the vigilance of my personal pilot Pierre Rey and, as a reward, I have decorated Pierre Rey with the Silver Ugandan Cross."

Moloro was now watching the guests, one of them in particular, with scarcely-concealed malicious pleasure. To Moloro this was like a play. And he already knew the script.

Amin's references to Rey were almost drowned by the exclamations and gasps of amazement. He waved for silence. "Five men have already paid the penalty and, by now, they are being educated by their seniors in the Muzimu. One of them—and I know this will pain you—was a man who enjoyed my personal trust, a man who would normally have been at this table tonight."

He paused dramatically and they stared at each other in wide-eyed silence. Through the evening they had been puzzled by the absence of Brigadier Apolo Brindeba. He had always been such a favourite and it had seemed strange that he, of all men, should not have been at the celebration. But they had all known better than to ask . . .

Moloro stroked the gun at his hip and Amin grinned as if savouring some gigantic joke. "The missing guest!" he said. "Perhaps some of you—perhaps especially one of you—felt disappointed that Brindeba was not able to be with us tonight. Eh, just a bit disappointed?"

"But what happened, Mr. President?" asked Kagwa. "How did they . . . ?"

Amin seemed not to hear. "Yes," he said. "Disappointed that Brindeba could not be here."

Suddenly he roared with laughter and the sound reverberated frighteningly around the room. "But I am not a man to let my friends be disappointed," he said. He wiped sweat from his brow with his sleeve. "No, I am not that sort of man. So, although he was misguided, I have made arrangements for Brindeba to be with us tonight."

Moloro, as if the words were a cue, stepped forward briskly and lifted the cover from the big silver tureen which was on a circular plinth in the middle of the table. In the dish, eyes open in the direction of Amin, was the severed head of Apolo Brindeba. The neck was decorated with a neatly-arranged ruff of white paper on which there were blotches of blood.

There was a shudder of revulsion around the table and one of the men clamped a hand to his mouth to stifle a scream.

Amin's voice was now mockingly courteous. "So, Brindeba, my friend, you have joined us. You are, as ever, welcome at my table for I bear you no ill-will. You were led astray by the evil that was in you but now you have been purified by death."

He glanced at his watch. "Perhaps you are lonely, my friend, without your three wives and your eight fine children. That is something I can understand for I too am a family man. To be separated from one's wives and children—that is indeed bad. And I am not a man who would wish badness on any friend so I have arranged for them to join you."

Another look at the watch. "Yes, my friend, in six minutes time they will be reunited with you. Their deaths will not be painful, not as yours was painful, and they will be grateful to be reunited with you."

Amin's eyes seemed to be full of genuine compassion. "I regret, I do deeply regret, that your own crossing had to be so unpleasant, but the suffering was necessary to cleanse you. And by now you will have absorbed the wisdom of my friends the Muzimu and once again, as it always was, you are my friend."

He was now getting more excited. His words were coming out faster and his baby-pink tongue was darting to the corners of his lips to capture the globules of spittle. "And, as a friend, Brindeba, there is one particular favour I must ask of you."

Amin stood and leaned forward towards the dead face. "There was one other was there not?' A quieter and almost wheedling voice. "There was a man who also had my trust. A man who has not yet been named but who was close enough to me to have been welcome here tonight."

A ghastly silence. Every man was watching Amin and Amin's eyes were fixed with hypnotic intensity on those of the dead man. "This man was your partner in evil. He, like you, was one of the misguided. And now— just before you are joined by your family—you will show him to me."

They were almost expecting words to come from the mouth of the dead man. But nothing. And Amin's rage erupted.

"Show him to me!" he bellowed. "Do as I order and show him!"

Moloro gave Amin the gun and Amin glowered around the table. "You will stay seated," he said. "All of you will stay seated. Those who have not been disloyal to me have nothing to fear."

Then, again, he was concentrating on Brindeba's head. "Now!" he shouted. "Your President is ordering you! Show me the guilty man!"

Moloro discreetly depressed a switch and the head started to gently revolve, as if the dish were mounted on a slow turn-table. The flickering of the candles gave the dead features a macabre semblance of life and the eyes of Brindeba seemed to reflect knowledge as they stared at each man in turn. "Nobody moves!" shouted Amin. "Nobody must move!" A complete circuit of the table. "Show him!" repeated Amin urgently. "Show him now!"

Still the head went on turning. Only now it was slower. And the men, transfixed by it, were repeating silent prayers. Then it stopped. For a moment Kagwa was mesmerised by the eyes fixed accusingly on him and then, realising the terrible implication, he started to rise. "No! Please . . . please . . . no! This is not right . . ."

His scream seemed to come simultaneously with the explosion from Amin's gun. Kagwa collapsed in his chair, a hole in the base of his forehead. His arms were outstretched as if nailed to an invisible cross. And the men near him were instantly aware of the foul smell as his sphincter muscle relaxed in death.

"Leave him!" ordered Amin. The instruction was superfluous for the others were too stunned to move. They just stared unbelievingly at Kagwa's corpse. Amin stretched forward and picked up Brindeba's head by the hair. Then he threw it at Kagwa's chest and it tumbled to rest in the lap of the dead man.

"They were together in life so it is fitting that they should be together in death," said Amin. "Now all of you can see what happens to those who try to defy the Muzimu."

He wiped his hands on the breast of his tunic. And, as if their movements were pre-ordained, the waiters bustled to remove the soup bowls and serve the next course.

Moloro watched his master with admiration. Such decisiveness! Such an impressive display of authority!

Amin again checked the time. "Brindeba will be happy by now," he said thoughtfully. "The firing squad will have done its work and his family will have joined him."

He sat down and grinned amiably at the men remaining around the table. "Come on—why so solemn?" he chided. "This is an evening for celebration, an evening to be enjoyed."

He cut himself a hunk of steak. "Apolo Brindeba was a family man," he said. "It is good to be a family man. My second wife—she is now again with child. So what an example I am setting you, eh? All the children I have fathered—don't they show I'm a powerful shooter?" He guffawed at his own joke. "Don't they go to prove that my aim is good?"

And, in the fullness of time, a detailed account of the events of the evening—with particular stress on the fate of Brindeba's innocent family—was filed in that Blue Dossier in Chicago.

* * *

They stripped the old man. They stripped him of his clothes and of his dignity. He was the mayor of a medium-sized town which, according to government spies, had given sanctuary to members of the anti-Amin guerilla organisation FRONASA—the Front for National Salvation.

There was no evidence to show that the old man had been personally involved but he was the mayor and so they were making a public exhibition of him. They bundled him, naked, out of his home and, in the centre of the town, they forced his family to watch while they roasted him with an oxy-acetylene blow-lamp. Then they lashed his left arm and his left leg to the rear of an army truck and the other arm and leg to the back of another vehicle. And, at the command of their officer, the drivers engaged their gears and stamped on their accelerators.

Next it was the turn of the mayor's married son who, like his father, was a respected Baganda Catholic. They chopped off his feet and then they chopped off his hands. As he lay screaming in the filth they cut off his penis. One of the soldiers laughed as he held it up for the crowd to see. And then he contemptuously threw it away.

19

One woman, distraught with grief, tried to run to the man to comfort him and a bayonet was plunged into her back.

These incidents, of course, were never reported in the Ugandan Press. They never officially happened.

Through the years of oppression the people of Uganda had learned to live with atrocities and sudden death. Men and women regularly went missing. They had, in the euphemism of the day, gone to Disappear Town . . .

By the summer of 1975 the International Commission of Jurists was claiming that nearly 25,000 black people were "missing" in Uganda. And it was a documented fact that many of those thousands had been murdered by the State. They had died by whipping and by starving, by drowning and by strangulation. Death came in so many imaginative and agonising forms.

And the facts, as far as they could be established, were carefully recorded in the Blue Dossier.

*　　*　　*

Stanton, the man from Chicago, Illinois, had grey eyes. They were bulbous and protruding—the result of a thyroid condition—and they made him seem rather like a paunchy bullfrog. He looked too well-scrubbed, too well-fed and too comfortably complacent. And appearances could never have been more deceptive. He deserved his reputation as one of the most lethal men in the most ruthless of games.

Now he was dressed with calculated casualness. Old sneakers with rope-soles, baggy slacks, and a sports shirt with a red cravat flopping over the collar.

His blue cap was new. Well, almost new. He had bought it before flying to England because it looked jaunty and nautical and he wanted the right acceptable image. He was, after all, playing the role of a yachting millionaire.

This Isle of Wight place—particularly this town of Cowes—impressed him enormously. This was where the top guys did their sailing. Guys like the Queen of England's husband and Edward Heath. And, even if he didn't exactly get to meet them, it was good to feel he was mixing with that sort of crowd. And this yacht *Pirouette*. All those around, in comparison, were no more than bath-tubs.

He skimmed the cap across the state-room at the row of gold-tipped hooks over the central port-hole. It missed and fell on the leather bench. "One of these days I'll do that right," he said. "It's a knack, y'know. Only a knack."

His companion, gigantic enough to dwarf any normal man, nodded politely. "Everything is a knack," he said. "Killing is a knack."

"Wrong, Theodor!"

Stanton poured himself a large whisky from the well-stocked cabinet and fixed a tomato juice with ice for Theodor.

"Completely and utterly wrong. Killing is a science. But this one has got to be more than just science. It's got to be a goddamned work of art."

Theodor accepted the juice. "How did you know?"

"Know?"

"About the drink. About me never touching it."

"It's my job to know. It's my job to know everything about you—and about everyone else on this mission. Believe me, Theodor, I know more about you than you know yourself."

He tasted his whisky, nodded approvingly, and topped up his glass. "If I couldn't honestly say that, my friend, I could never have asked you to join us."

"Do you know the truth, the real truth, about how my wife died?"

"Naturally."

"But that is not possible. My colleagues in the police force—even they did not know the real truth."

"I know it," said Stanton. "And I know exactly how you felt."

Theodor seemed disconcerted. "Then Gottschalk must have told you and he had no right. It was a confidence . . ."

Stanton sprawled back in one of the huge armchairs and impatiently gestured for Theodor to do the same. "You've read the Blue File?"

"Of course."

"Good. We've wasted enough time." Stanton's voice was crisper now and more authoritative. "The others will be here shortly and, in view of your special responsibilities, there are matters we must discuss."

"There are," said Theodor sombrely. "Particularly the matter of Moloro." His socks were too short and, as he relaxed in his chair, the tops of his ankles showed starkly white. "That's not going to be easy, you know. Not as easy as you seem to think."

"I hope I didn't give the impression that I considered it easy," said Stanton. "It's difficult and it's goddamned dangerous. The whole job is. Slip up just once when you're in Uganda and there'll be a bullet in your head—if you're lucky."

Theodor fished a cube of ice out of his drink and crunched it between his teeth. "It's not the danger I'm talking about," he said. "It's the practicality. Me, a German—officially just a tourist in the country—taking over the job of Amin's chief bodyguard . . . well, it's stretching our luck . . ."

"Follow the plan Theodor," said Stanton. "Just follow the plan. And remember—you idolised Hitler."

"I've never hated any man so vehemently . . ."

"Don't change the subject. For the purpose of this exercise you idolised him."

Theodor nodded. "Worshipped him," he said. He drained his glass. "This information about Amin's pilot—the Frenchman, Pierre Rey. Is it known to Amin?"

Stanton got up to fix more drinks. Whisky for himself and a juice for Theodor. "Rey has been careful to keep it from him. He knows it would cost him his job."

"And there's no doubt about its accuracy?"

"A rock-solid source in Paris."

"Sorry, I should have known better than to ask."

"Don't be sorry," said Stanton. "If you've got any doubts, let them spill out now. It'll be too late when you get there . . ."

*   *   *

There were few people in the Three Pilchards pub near the waterfront at Cowes. Just a small group of regular lunchtime drinkers at the bar and, in the far corner, two men talking in confidentially low voices.

"This feller Stanton—he's sussed us out pretty thoroughly, hasn't he." Weaver took a gulp of his beer and burped with vulgar satisfaction. He took another gulp as if to wash away the taste of the burp. "Oh yes, every bloody wart—he's got a note of it somewhere. But what about him? You know much about him?"

Weaver's intensity made Lajeba feel vaguely disconcerted. It was the way Weaver looked at him—or maybe the way Weaver did not look at him. He could never be certain which it was. The Australian's glass left eye—that was the trouble.

Usually it was rigidly fixed but just occasionally, by contracting the muscles of his socket, Weaver could twitch it a little to give it a semblance of life. All very disconcerting.

"I don't know a great deal," admitted Lajeba. "He doesn't talk much, not about himself."

"So I've found. He's tight, that one. Tight as a virgin's arse."

Lajeba bit some dead skin from the edge of one of his finger-nails and spat it to the ground. "I understand he was, for some years, quite senior in the CIA."

"Not *quite* senior," said Weaver. "*Very* senior. Great specialist in dirty tricks. That's why he's heading up this scheme. I checked as far as I could and it seems he retired—as much as a feller like that ever does retire—about three years ago. But don't get any wrong ideas. This is no CIA job. This is one boy who wouldn't touch it if it was—not even for the cash we're getting."

"It's not just the money," said Lajeba. "It's for my country, for the whole continent of Africa."

"Sure, it's for the whole wide world," said Weaver sardonically. "But you'll still take the money."

"I'll take it. But only because I'll need it to survive afterwards . . ."

"You don't have to explain to me, old son . . ."

"I'm not explaining," said Lajeba defensively. "I'm just saying. But, still, it feels wrong somehow—accepting money for killing a man."

"I killed a man once." Weaver was casual, anxious to cool the tension he could feel mounting in the black man. "Back in Melbourne. I strangled him."

"For money?"

"No, not for money. Not for any bloody reason as it turned out. I just picked the wrong poor bastard."

Lajeba nibbled away more of his finger-nail skin. "Perhaps he deserved it."

"No, he was the wrong poor bastard." A look at his watch. "Come on, just time for one more before we get that boat. Same again?"

Lajeba thanked him. And while Weaver was getting the drinks Lajeba pondered on the outlandish adventure to which he was now committed. The background—or rather the pieces of it he had been able to jigsaw together—was almost surrealistically impossible. Yet it happened to be true.

Stanton had been commissioned by a group of anonymous millionaires to recruit the team and organise the enterprise. They were from a whole mix of countries, these background men, and—as far as Lajeba could establish—they were not motivated by national considerations nor by the standard suspicions between East and West. They just had a genuine concern for all human life. They were, as they saw it, trying to save the world. That was why, for this one-off enterprise, they had given themselves a secret syndicate name—Sanity International.

Lajeba suspected that their fears were pitched too high. He did not see how the carnage could possibly envelop the world. It was quite out of perspective. But he did know how his own beloved Uganda was being destroyed, and that was why he had agreed so willingly to co-operate.

Twenty minutes later a blue motor-boat was whisking him and Weaver out to the yacht *Pirouette*.

"Good," said Stanton. "Only two to come now—just Carter and the girl."

* * *

Porters were shouting angrily at her—ordering her to stand clear of the train. But the woman, a dark little whirl of agitated determination, ignored them and scrambled on board as it was pulling away. Then she had difficulty in closing the door and the man, the only other person in the first-class carriage, hurried across to help.

"Thank you. That is most kind." Her accent was a foreign one which he could not place.

"You can get killed that way," he said.

She shrugged, completely composed now and relaxed in her corner seat. "You can get killed so many ways."

Hardly the expected answer. But then, he decided, she seemed an unexpected type. Attractive but not exactly beautiful. Certainly not as beautiful as most of the girls he had bedded. Yet there was something . . .

Yes, that was it. Her air of vitality. Her vitality and the quiet self-assurance she radiated.

She refused his offer of a cigarette but took a tiny silver box from her handbag and deftly poured a trickle of snuff on to the back of her left hand.

"I used to smoke too many cigarettes but they are bad for one." A delicate sniff as she inhaled the powder and she dabbed her nose with a handkerchief. "My brother always says they are bad for one."

They were now well out of Waterloo Station and the squalid confusion of south London was sliding past.

"Your brother is right." He lit his cigarette. "You going to Southampton?"

"First Southampton and then the Island of Wight."

"Me too. Business trip." A sudden thought. He could rarely resist the prospect, however tenuous, of a new woman. "Maybe we could explore together tonight. Have a meal and so on. I've got a dreary meeting this afternoon but I should be free about seven . . ."

She smiled. "Could it be—Mr. Carter—that we will be at the same dreary meeting?"

That hit him off-guard. "How do you know my name?"

"Then you are Mr. Carter?"

"I asked a question."

She yawned as if it was supremely unimportant. "Yellow hair, blue eyes—and that dimple thing in your chin. Stanton told me."

"It's called a cleft. The dimple thing—it's called a cleft." He studied her with suspicion. "Stanton didn't mention any woman. Not to me."

"I'm more anonymous than you, Mr. Carter. I have to be."

"So who are you?"

"You can call me Barbra. It's not my name, but you can call me it."

"And your real name?"

She shook her head impatiently. "The authorities in

Warsaw—they are less understanding than the authorities here. You call me Barbra. It is best."

"Okay, so it's Barbra. And how do you fit in the team?"

"I'm a technical expert, Mr. Carter. Let us leave it at that."

"And why are you doing it? It's bloody risky, y'know."

"Because badness must be stopped."

"Crap!"

"Please?"

"Crap—it's an English expression. It means you're not exactly telling the truth. People do this sort of job for money or they do it for revenge. They do it because they're greedy or because they hate somebody's guts. They do it because they're frightened or because they need a thrill or because they're half bloody mad. But they don't do it for where's-your-bloody-halo idealism."

"Crap." She fondled the word with her lips as if savouring a pleasant new taste. "That's a funny word. It is English colloquialism, yes?"

"That's right—colloquial."

"It is good for one to learn colloquial English. It is better for my conversation." She helped herself to more snuff. "How did your nose get broken?"

Her directness made him grin as he fingered the kink. "Would you believe boxing?"

Now it was her turn to grin. "Boxing, perhaps, with a jealous husband?"

"Jesus!" he said in mock anger. "That bloody Stanton! He has been rattling on, hasn't he?"

Her eyes were teasing. "Perhaps he was just warning me not to be too distracted by your good English looks."

"And perhaps he should mind his own good American business. Anyway, it wasn't a husband. Just a boyfriend—in Singapore."

"My brother broke a man's nose once," said Barbra. "In Posnan."

"Because of a woman?"

"No—because the man was a German. He was a German and he had a loud voice."

"Was he pissed? Your brother, I mean. Was he pissed?"

"What is pissed?"

"Another one for your collection," said Carter. "Another colloquialism. It means inebriated . . . you know, drunk."

"Oh no, he was not drunk," she replied. "It was because of the war. The Germans—they did bad things in the war. Terrible, terrible things . . ."

Christ, thought Carter. Doesn't she know she's being partnered with the Kraut?

The hovercraft hurtled them across Southampton Water and the blue motor-boat was waiting for them at West Cowes. Stanton welcomed them effusively to *Pirouette*. "Come and join the party," he said. "We're all ready to start."

*　　*　　*

Canvas chairs were scattered around the sun-deck of the *Pirouette*. In one corner, near the box of rag-worm bait, was an impressive selection of gaffs and sea-rods. Stanton waved towards the drinks table by the hatchway leading aft to the state-room. "Help yourselves, folks," he said. "And act as if this is a fun party. There's to be no discussion until we're right away from land."

He took his position at the wheel and, as he was about to start the engines, he caught just a snatch of the conversation behind him.

Barbra's voice: "Very little, please, for me. I do not wish to get passed."

And Carter's: "Pissed. The word is pissed."

Barbra again: "Thank you—I am grateful." A pause—and then: "That is an English colloquialism, you know, Mr. Lajeba. It means drunk or inebriated."

Then Lajeba, speaking with immense courtesy: "Yes —I have encountered the word before."

All else was lost to Stanton as the powerful Commodore diesel engines roared into life and *Pirouette*'s bows lifted high from the water. Soon, in the distance, they could see the church steeple and the pier at Ryde . . . the beaches of Sandown and Shanklin . . . and, eventually they were in the loneliness of the deep waters. When Stanton cut the engines the silence was as tangible as a wall around them. In that silence they were aware of the small noises. The screeching of distant gulls . . . water flopping listlessly against the sides . . . the rhythmic groaning of a deck-board under pressure. And *Pirouette* rocked in the gentle swell.

"A couple of old wrecks down there somewhere," said Stanton. "If I've figured it right, we're just about on top of them."

Weaver twitched his false eye. "And you reckon they've got squatters, eh?"

"They always have. Ling . . . cod . . . pollack . . . it's all down there waiting for you."

They already knew the routine. Carter, Weaver and Lajeba would do the real fishing, all from the same side of the yacht. Theodor would be with them, catching mackerel for them to cut into bait. Stanton and Barbra, the experts on international politics, would stand behind them—just casually watching, it would seem to any distant observer. That was the way the conference was to be conducted.

Theodor was now baiting his multi-hooked line and Stanton was pacing the deck behind the line of seated men. "I want to stress again—we are not in this for vengeance."

Carter glanced over his shoulder. "Of course, that belongs to the Lord."

A frown and a flicker of annoyance on Stanton's face. "I didn't catch that?"

"It's a saying." Carter was still fiddling with his tackle. "Vengeance is mine, saith the Lord."

"Fascinating," said Stanton. His bullfrog eyes were more bleak than usual. "As I was saying . . . we're not out to punish for the crimes of the past. What's done is done. We've merely analysed the past—as you've seen in the blue dossiers—to help us get the future in better perspective."

Theodor's first tangle of mackerel was now convulsing from the water, iridescent and shimmeringly luminous in the sun. Weaver and Lajeba bloodied their hands slashing the fishes into bits.

"The future—that's our only concern," said Stanton. "And the facts of that future are frightening."

All the lines were now in the water.

"The whole African continent is ready to explode. And that would throw East and West into the most catastrophic conflict."

"Nuclear war," added Barbra. "Without question."

Lajeba was steadying his rod with one hand and pensively nibbling at the finger-nail skin of the other. He was risking more than any of them for he was on the staff of the Ugandan High Commission in London. Soon, his tour over, he would be returning to Government House in Entebbe.

He spat out the skin. "Every month the President . . . he is becoming more obsessive," he said. "He is determined to lead black Africa against the white regimes of Rhodesia and South Africa . . ."

"So what's new?" There was a jeer in Carter's voice. "That's his old hobby horse. He was spouting that stuff back in July 1975 at the OAU ministerial council . . ."

"His determination to smash those regimes is even stronger now . . ."

"Well, there's a lot in those regimes that needs smashing," said Carter.

"Not at the risk of destroying the world," interrupted Stanton sharply.

Lajeba was now concentrating on his taut line and, as if temporarily oblivious to the conversation, was reeling in a medium-sized pollack. Theodor gaffed it and it looked almost comically indignant as it flapped urgently against the boards of the deck.

Stanton glanced at Barbra. "Do a bit of under-lining for us will you. Friend Carter seems to need it."

Barbra was about to take a pinch of snuff. She completed the action unhurriedly and dabbed at her nose before responding: "Amin will have far more support than most of the white nations realise. Even Nyerere of Tanzania has stated that Rhodesia will have to be liberated by force. And he is a moderate by African standards—a man who has denounced Amin as a murderer."

She was now talking directly at Carter. "War against Rhodesia will involve the butchering of countless thousands of people. And it will lead to far worse."

Through all the talk, the fishing continued. It had to look right. There were other small boats towards the horizon and it was just possible they were being watched through glasses. Stanton was a perfectionist . . .

Another pollack for Lajeba. A modest cod for Weaver. And now there was an angry convulsion on Carter's line. Something big and very active. Carter started working earnestly with his reel. Barbra knew that, despite appearances, she still had their attention and she went on: "The Tanzanian capital, Dar es Salaam, is a central base for terrorist organisations which—in a crusade against the whites—would unite with Amin. Millions of pounds worth of weaponry— Mig fighters, light tanks, B40 rocket launchers and so on—are now moving through the Dar docks from China and Russia . . ."

"And in addition to that," said Stanton, "more than 2,000 Ugandan soldiers, airmen and technicians have been sent for training in Eastern Europe."

Weaver was pushing half a mackerel on his hook. He had snagged himself and, on his wrist, his own blood was mixed with that of the dead fish. "That's a two-way traffic, isn't it?" He cast with the deftness of an expert. "Barbra here's just one example. Going to Uganda as a technical advisor."

"That's why she's in this team," said Stanton.

Carter was now standing, his muscles straining against the fury of his catch. The fish was bucking violently and, occasionally, breaking the surface. And Barbra carried on talking as evenly as if she were in a lecture-theatre: "Nyerere and the others—even if they were reluctant to link with Amin—would have very little choice. Kenya . . . Zambia . . . Tanzania . . . not one of them has a strong official army and they have virtually no air forces . . ."

She gave no indication of seeing anything incongruous about the apparent preoccupation of her audience—with Theodor tumbling another catch of writhing mackerel into the messy visceral heap on the deck.

"With the backing of Gaddafi of Libya—a fellow Moslem who, as you know, has an oil income of more than £1,000 million a year—Amin could sweep through those countries."

"Correct," said Stanton. "They'd be forced to fall into line."

Theodor chopped up more mackerel. "The Prussia of East Africa," he said thoughtfully.

"The Prussia of all Africa," corrected Stanton. "Potentially, at any rate. Then there are other considerations. Ethiopia, for instance. Haile Selassie, as a Coptic Christian, would undoubtedly have opposed Amin. Now, with Selassie gone, the position of Ethiopia is very different.

"And Somalia—another Moslem country being armed by the Soviets—would also throw its support behind Amin."

Carter's line snapped. "Sod!" he exclaimed. He started pulling in the drifting limpness of line. "Best

32

catch yet and the bastard breaks away." He rested his rod and sat down. "What about Nigeria?" he queried. "The richest state in black Africa."

Stanton was beginning to dislike Carter. There was an unpleasant arrogance about the man. And, anyway, the reaction of Nigeria in any black-white war had been detailed in the red dossier. Carter had studied the dossier. He should know.

"What about Nigeria?" demanded Stanton.

Carter got up to fix himself a drink. "It's simply that I feel we're assessing it wrongly," he said. "General Gowon was friendly with Amin. Damn it all, he was with Amin in Kampala at the time he was deposed." He downed his drink and poured another. "So look at it logically. Is it likely that the men who threw him out are going to line up alongside Amin?"

"It is highly likely," said Lajeba unexpectedly. "Gowon was one of the most stable heads of state in black Africa. He'd lived through the horror of Biafra. He'd seen the nightmare that brought and he would never have been a party to setting Africa aflame . . ."

"But his successors—they're a very different bunch," said Stanton. "They'll want to share the glory of helping to sweep the white man out of Africa. And Nigeria, remember, has a standing army of more than a quarter of a million men—and a military budget of more than £280 million a year."

So they talked on. They talked about the aid which Amin would get from the powerful guerilla organisations such as the Zimbabwe African National Union. They talked about how the independence of Mozambique had enabled terrorist gangs to establish camps right down Rhodesia's eastern border—and how the Cubans were eager to build on their triumphs in Angola. And, far more important, they talked about the inevitable intervention of the giant powers.

The Eastern bloc would continue to give enormous help to black Africa. The Russians and the Chinese would be competing to extend their spheres of influence. And the huge mineral wealth of South Africa—copper, uranium, iron-ore, chrome, diamonds and gold—would be just one of the many prizes.

The United States and her allies would be compelled to counter this aid—first with materials and money and, eventually, with fighting men.

"And it would be a matter of time before one side or the other considered that a nuclear strike was justified to end the carnage," said Stanton. "Don't kid yourselves it couldn't happen. It was my country that set the pattern."

*   *   *

Weaver's shark was the catch of the day. It was a porbeagle, just over seven feet long, but Weaver showed no pride in it. "There's no such thing as a big fish, not in these waters," he said. "You ought to see the things we get around Australia. Mantas with wingspans of twenty feet or more. They can weigh more than three thousand pounds, some of them. And when you're fighting a fish that size—boy, you're really fighting!"

"Let's get back to business, shall we?" said Stanton brusquely. "There'll be plenty of time for fishing stories when the job's done. As I was saying . . . it is imperative that this is never recognised as a deliberate killing."

"We can't risk him becoming a martyr," added Barbra.

"Correct," said Stanton. "That could give added impetus to his aims and, with one of his fanatical henchmen taking over, the bang could come even faster. That's why I've gone to such trouble to devise the accident. And that's also why we're taking on the job of protecting Amin from all other assassination attempts. If necessary, we will kill those trying to kill him."

"Rather ironic, isn't it?" said Carter.

"Perhaps," said Stanton. "But if any of them were to kill him, the results could be as disastrous as if we were to kill him the wrong way. It must be recognised, beyond doubt, as an accident."

Carter was still not convinced. "I've got to hand it to you," he said. "Your plan is brilliant. But it's far too complicated. Unnecessarily complicated."

They had stopped fishing by now and were tidying the decks before starting back for Cowes. "You have a better plan?" There was tetchy hostility in Stanton's voice.

"Well, we could do it far more easily by smuggling just one man into Uganda—one of the silver-stamp men from Kelantan."

"I'm not following you."

"Kelantan. On the east coast of Malaysia . . ."

"I was hoping for elucidation—not a geography lesson."

Carter suppressed the temptation to flare back. He spoke slowly, as if he was explaining something to a small child: "These men, these men in Kelantan, they're professional killers whose work is never detected. They use tiny silver blades, no bigger than postage-stamps, which they flick through the air with lethal accuracy.

"They catch the victim right in the middle of the back of the neck and the blade severs the spinal chord. Instantaneous death and—here's the beautiful part—the victim shows all the symptoms of having suffered a heart-attack. It's accepted, you see, as natural death."

"And that, you feel, is superior to my plan?"

"I do. It's so neat and uncluttered. All this business of Weaver and me going to Istanbul to abduct Marcel Rey and his wife . . . it's not necessary. You're just promoting a simple operation into a spectacular." He lit a cigarette. "And I'll tell you something else about the silver-stamp men. Their little blades go in so fast, and they're so fine, that the flesh seals immediately they've gone through. There's no visible sign of them . . ."

Stanton was beginning to regret having included this Englishman in the team. He was too independent and opinionated. Yet the reports on him had been good . . .

Carter had intelligence, strength and courage. He had proved in other spheres that his loyalty, once given, was absolute. He was also a highly-experienced man, having accomplished a variety of hazardous missions in many regions of the world. It was on one of those missions, presumably, that he had learned about the silver-stamp killers and—quite possibly—had even hired one of them.

Only one flaw was documented in Carter's file which was locked away in Chicago. He was an inveterate womaniser. He had, in fact, been expelled from his public school because of the pregnancy of a fifth-former at the nearby convent. That, however, hardly seemed a character fault which could have any bearing on this particular operation—and yet Stanton felt uneasy.

Perhaps, after all, he had made an error over Carter. He tried to smother the thought. "I would endorse that method if I were planning to kill a bricklayer's mate," he said. "I would endorse it if I were planning to kill any one of thousands of people. In fact, I compliment you on offering us a rather original method of instant death. However, for our purpose—for the killing of the President of Uganda—it would be worse than useless. In fact, to be brutally frank, it would be downright stupid."

The others—Barbra, Weaver, Lajeba and Theodor —had now stowed away the fish and the tackle. They were grouped around the bar-table, silent and perturbed by this personality clash. Carter flushed angrily and Stanton raised a hand warningly. "Now let me finish. A simple explanation of a heart attack would not be automatically accepted in the case of a man like Amin. There would be an inquiry. There would be an autopsy. And then what would happen? Your little blade would be discovered—that's what would happen. It would be discovered and it would be realised that the death had been caused by an assassin."

He paused. "Need I go on?"

Carter shook his head. "Sorry," he said. "I'll be with Weaver on that plane to Istanbul . . ."

* * *

Another straggle of guerillas, armed with Russian AK47 automatic rifles, was moving through Zambia and across the Zambesi River—heading for the sanctuary of the Mountains of Mavuradonha.

They were some of the 1,000 black youths who had recently left Rhodesia for secret training at the base called Knongwa in Tanzania. And on the mountains, hidden from the spotter aircraft of the Rhodesian security forces, they would join the others already massing over the tribal trust land of north-eastern Rhodesia.

Soon they would be joining in the terror raids on the families of the white farmers. They, like others before them, would leave a trail of mutilated corpses and devastated buildings. And this would be just a tiny taste of the horror which could convulse the whole continent and threaten the whole world.

* * *

Amin was making another Presidential broadcast on Radio Uganda:

"Adolph Hitler, as I have explained to the United Nations, was right about the Jews. They were the leeches of Germany, sucking her blood and sapping her strength. He was right to destroy them and so, in order to honour this man of vision, a statue is to be erected to him in the middle of Kampala. The men and the women of Uganda will pay homage to that statue.

"Today the white people, all the white people, are the Jews of Africa. They exploit and tyrannise our black brothers. The time is now coming for the yoke of oppression to be thrown off. The time is now coming for the black men of Africa, the true and rightful owners of Africa, to unite . . ."

*   *   *

A battered old American car, serving as a taxi, took Carter from Istanbul airport to his hotel near Karakoy Square. Weaver, travelling separately, checked into a nearby hotel. Operation Amin had started.

CHAPTER 2

The earthquake which shuddered across eastern Turkey in September, 1975, brought death and destruction on an appalling scale. It also exposed an unexpected pattern of tools and cooking-pots and primitive ornaments from a long-forgotten past. Historians and archaeologists were excited by reports of these finds and, long after the burying of the dead and the re-building of the villages, they were still arriving in small groups from many parts of the world.

Marcel Rey had just spent three months in the region with his wife Yvette. Three very successful months. Now his treasures, many intended for museums in France, were tagged and packed. And the Reys were relaxing for a while in Istanbul.

Their plans for the immediate future were vague. They had not decided how long they would stay in Istanbul or whether, before returning home, they would go on a sight-seeing jaunt around Greece.

It really didn't matter. They had no time-table to keep and they were answerable to no-one. And, for the moment, all Yvette wanted to do was to pamper herself—to enjoy the stimulation of the city and the luxuries of a good hotel. She was not as enthusiastic as her husband about antiquities and she felt that, after all that time in the wilderness of the east, she deserved a break. The heat and the flies and the loneliness—it had all been far worse than she had expected. There hadn't even been a decent-looking man within a radius of fifty miles . . .

As she stepped from the shower she admired herself in the full-length mirror. It was just as well, she thought, about that baby. She'd been upset at the time but, really, it was just as well. Babies could play havoc with a girl's figure. Yvette Rey, not without cause, was pleased with her figure.

She extended her arms, holding the hotel towel like a pink drape so that all she could see of herself in the mirror was her head and the tops of her shoulders. Then, her arms still out, she let the towel drop to the floor. This was a game she had often played. Trying to imagine herself into the mind of some strange man . . . trying to capture his thoughts as he suddenly saw her nakedness. There had been so few men since her marriage . . .

While she was dressing she thought, as she had thought so many times, that marrying Marcel had been a terrible mistake. He was dependable and good-natured and loving. But he was so bloody boring.

Their visit to the Topkapi Palace—that had just about epitomised the relationship between them. They had seen the same sights and heard the same sounds—yet, all the time, they had been in completely different worlds.

"Just look at the designs on that door," he'd said. "Do you realise that some of them belong to the twelfth century B.C.? And one of them—there, that one, in fact—is actually Phrygian in origin . . ."

Drivel . . . drivel . . . on and on . . .

She'd been more interested in how the Palace wood-humpers—strong and handsome men from the Anatolian mountains—used to have their heads clamped in special collars, to stop them looking left or right, when their work took them into the harem. And she'd idly wondered if the maidens of the harem might not have fancied these men . . . if only as a change . . .

"Quite incredible, isn't it? Before this church was

dedicated to St. Irene it was used as a temple to Aphrodite and excavations have now revealed that . . ."

So who cares? Who bloody cares?

What about the interesting things? That oddly-shaped stone where they used to show off the heads of executed men . . . the fountain where the high executioners would wash the blood off their axes and scimitars . . .

"It was here, you appreciate, that the second oecumenical council met under Theodosius in the year 381 . . ."

Dear Lord . . . forgive us . . . and deliver us from all tedium . . .

As they were having dinner that evening she tried to needle him over money. She was never prepared to let him forget how little he earned, how little he had of his own. Their style of life . . . the way they travelled . . . they could not possibly afford it if it were not for the money she'd inherited from her father.

"That's the real reason you married me, isn't it?" she said. "It wasn't me or my body you wanted. It was the money we'd get one day from my father."

He smiled that infuriatingly tolerant smile of his and he shook his head. "Now come along, Yvette," he said gently. "Don't let's go over all that again. You know it's nonsense."

But she had said it so often that she was beginning to half-believe it.

He sipped his wine and changed the subject. "You think I've made the right decision? About Pierre."

She shrugged. "It's up to you, isn't it? It's your decision."

"But do you think it's the right one? It does concern you as well, you know."

"I've told you before, Marcel—you've got to do what you think is right."

"Well, anyway, I'm doing it. I've signed the papers and it's all fixed. You can hardly change your mind when you've signed the papers."

"No-one's asking you to." Her tone conveyed the depths of her disinterest.

"You do like Pierre, don't you?" There was just a suggestion of reproach in his voice. "I used to think that, once, you were quite fond of him."

She looked at him steadily, trying to divine some hidden meaning in the comment. "And what, precisely, is that suppose to mean?"

"Just what it says—that's all. You used to seem fond of him."

"There's only one person who's really fond of your brother Pierre," she replied. "And that's Pierre."

They left the hotel separately the following morning.

Marcel was looking forward to exploring the mosque of Ramazan Efendi, near the Kocamustafa Palace, which was built in 1586 by Sinan. He did not realise he was being followed by the Englishman Carter.

And Yvette, off on a souvenir-hunt around the Grand Bazaar, did not notice the man tagging behind her. He was an Australian with only one eye.

*　　*　　*

Even Theodor, for all his height, was dwarfed by the ebony immigration official at Entebbe. The man was glowering at him, hostile and suspicious. "Why you come to Uganda?"

"To see your beautiful country," said Theodor politely. "I have heard so much about it."

"You a tourist?"

"That's right. A tourist. I've just retired and I've decided to treat myself . . ."

"Tourist." The man scratched his head with a ballpoint pen. "How long you stay?"

"Three weeks or so . . ."

"Three weeks," said the man. "You want to stay longer and you make new application." He rubber-stamped a purple visa into Theodor's passport. It read:

"Permitted to enter Uganda on condition that the holder does not remain longer than (here there was a gap) and does not take any employment, paid or unpaid, without the permission of the Principal Immigration Officer."

Then the man frowned in concentration as, in a laborious and child-like hand, he wrote the words "three weeks" into the gap. He handed back the passport without a smile and waved Theodor through.

Theodor did not have a particularly lively sense of humour. Life, to him, was a serious business and he was also very conscious of the dangers into which he was moving. But, even so, he was wryly amused by the wording of the visa. What, he wondered, would be the reaction of the Principal Immigration Officer if he—Theodor—did seek "permission" to do the job he was intending to do? "It's only a small job. Hardly worth mentioning, really. I'm just here to kill your President . . ."

As he waited outside the airport building for a taxi, he saw Lajeba being escorted to a car by a man in uniform. They had been on the same flight from Gatwick but had ignored each other and now there was no flicker of recognition between them.

"You will first take me to Bugambe," Lajeba was saying to his driver. "I have to pay my respects to my father."

Overhead, Theodor noticed the Russian jet preparing for descent. Barbra, he knew, would be on board. In a few minutes the assassination team in Uganda would be complete.

By the time Barbra, and other members of the technical-aid team, had gone through the airport formalities, Theodor was almost at his hotel in Kampala. And, about the same time, Stanton was busy on the telephone in his Chicago office. He was giving final instructions to a man in Cairo:

"It's very simple. They've both been written and

addressed in Marcel Rey's handwriting . . . the job's been done by an expert. All you have to do is post the picture-card tomorrow and the letter in four days' time . . . yes, I have heard from Istanbul. It's definitely on for today."

* * *

An angry protest of pigeons, more dirty and dejected than any pigeons she had seen before, flurried around Yvette as she strolled towards the Nur-u-Osmaniya gate which led into the confused and narrow labyrinths of the covered Grand Bazaar.

It smelled of dust in the tree-shaded courtyard. Of dust and flowers and old, decaying fruit.

The pigeons seemed irritated at being disturbed in their scavenging—just as she was already starting to feel irritated by the pleading persistance of the urchin street-pedlars.

"You French? French people very good. All French people my friends. You like these belts—huh? Very good belts. I make you good price . . ."

It was almost uncanny—the way these boys, touting their beads and bangles and leather oddments, could always identify the nationality of a foreigner with such unerring accuracy. They had known with Yvette before she had said a word. No question of thinking of her, possibly, as a German or an American. It was as if she was wearing a placard with "Made in France" across her chest.

A skinny and limping boy—aged perhaps ten or eleven—with tattered clothing and huge, imploring eyes. Would she let him clean her shoes for one lira?

"No," she said. "Go away." And she felt guilty as she said it. He looked so full of woe.

"Madame, please . . . please, madame . . . I have no father and no mother. I have nine little brothers and a sister . . . not one lira, madame . . . just two cigarettes . . . please, just two cigarettes and I clean your shoes good . . ."

She could still hear him, beseeching plaintively after her, as she turned right into the jewellery section of the Bazaar.

"Just one cigarette madame, that's all . . . I'm hungry, I have no food . . . just give me one cigarette . . ."

And now, as she wandered through the cluttered alleys of clamour and mesmeric gaudiness, she was accosted by fresh swarms of wandering hawkers and shop-door touts. Tee-shirts and Turkish flags . . . glass-bejewelled daggers and bars of chocolate . . . rugs and carrier-bags and baleful stuffed-camel toys . . . all of this, and so much more, was being urged on her. And suddenly she was surprised to hear her own name.

A man who had come from behind was gripping her elbow. "Madame Rey?" he asked again. He was wearing a blue open-necked shirt under a neat light-weight suit and he looked respectable. But his eyes didn't seem normal. There was something odd about the way they were staring at her. One of them, the left one, had a disconcerting intensity . . .

"That's me," she said. "But who are you?"

"Thank God I've found you," said Weaver. "It was just a chance . . . your husband said you were probably here somewhere . . ."

"My husband?" Yvette jerked her elbow free. "I don't know you . . . I don't know what you're talking about."

"I'm sorry—let me start again," said Weaver. "My name's Black. Jim Black. I work at the hospital down by the Galata Bridge. Now I don't want you to be alarmed but I'm afraid there's been a bit of an accident . . ."

A youth in a red-and-yellow tunic was trying to draw her attention to an ugly toy monkey bouncing on a length of elastic.

"What do you mean, accident?"

"Your husband . . . he got hit by a van."

"Oh, no . . ."

The monkey was now being jerked between them and the youth was demanding money.

"He's not badly hurt. It's just his legs. They're both broken."

Yvette roughly pushed the monkey-seller away. "Mr. Black . . . I've got to get to him."

"He's asking for you," said Weaver. "I've got a car. Come on."

He took her hand and she ran with him to the exit. The car, with a Turk at the wheel, hurtled them up the congested, humpy road and then steeply down past the Selimiye Barracks and the Central Station towards the Maritime Bank near the edge of the water.

They swerved to miss a viciously over-loaded cart which was being pulled by a threadbare mule; and an ancient man, perched high on the load, swore gummily at them. And then, in a swirl of dust, they skidded to a halt just beyond the Bank. Yvette, even in her agitation, was surprised by the squat and unfriendly building at which they had arrived. There were two windows, high in its dun-coloured front wall, and both were fortressed with iron bars. "This doesn't look much like a hospital."

"It's a small one." Weaver was now hustling her to the partly-open door. "A private one. Come on—quickly."

And, as the heavy door was slammed behind them, Yvette could hear the tearing of gears as the car began speeding away.

That same car, a short time later, was parked in Kocamustafa Pasha Avenue. And, inside the nearby mosque of Ramazan Efendi, an Englishman who claimed his name was Richards was speaking softly but urgently to Marcel Rey. He had yellow hair, this Englishman, and a distinctive cleft in his chin. "No, your wife's not badly hurt," he was saying. "It's only her legs. They're both broken . . ."

The two men retrieved their shoes at the entrance of the mosque and the car raced them to the dun-coloured building standing between the Maritime Bank and the Galata Bridge.

Strong arms grabbed Marcel as Carter—the man calling himself Richards—bustled him into the dimness of the building. He fought wildly but Carter was helping his unseen attackers, twisting his arms painfully behind his back. A pad, impregnated with some acrid chemical, was clamped over his nose and mouth and the room seemed to blur and tilt at a crazy angle. His brain was drowning in mists . . . his legs were uncontrollable foam-rubber . . . and he felt himself choking as he collapsed into the blackness . . .

Yvette and Marcel, still unconscious, were securely trussed and gagged. Carter nodded with satisfaction. "Get them crated and on board before I get back," he said. "I'm going to check them out of their hotel."

There were two Turks, also on the pay-roll of Sanity International, to help Weaver. They were resourceful men, men who occasionally supplemented their income with a little smuggling. The job should not take long . . .

A fluster of tourists was harassing the desk-clerk at the hotel and he hardly had time to attend to Carter. "My name's Rey," said Carter. "Room fifty-seven. My key please. And get my bill made up, will you? My wife and I are leaving."

He quickly packed the Rey's belongings and tipped a boy to carry them to a taxi.

As he settled the account, he said to the clerk: "If anyone tries to contact me, please tell them I've gone to Cairo. The Hotel Gezi, Cairo."

"Certainly, Mr. Rey," said the clerk. "Have a good flight."

By the time Carter reached the waterfront, the Reys were already locked in separate cabins in the unprepossessing tramp-steamer and men were busy hoisting the official cargo on board.

Carter was pleased with the smoothness, so far, of the operation. "Well," he said. "Morocco, here we come!"

"Let's just hope that Cherif's got everything ready there for us," said Weaver.

"Don't worry about it," said Carter. "He's a good man. Stanton picked him personally . . ."

*　　*　　*

Pierre Rey's home was a tucked-away, low-roofed bugalow on Mengo Hill—which, in the days of the Kabakas, had been regarded as the royal hill—but it took him barely fifteen minutes to drive into the heart of Kampala.

In fact, he did little more than sleep at the bungalow. Most of his time, when he was not needed by Amin, was spent at the Metropolitan Hotel. He ate there, drank there, and, just occasionally, picked up women there.

The Metropolitan was the hub of social life in Kampala, the most popular venue for relaxing politicians and for foreign visitors. The bars and other public rooms were plushly comfortable. The service was obsequiously efficient. And, even in the times of shortages, the food was always excellent.

Rey was bored. Bored with his own company. There was only one other white person in the bar, an exceptionally tall German tourist who was sadly drinking tomato-juice. Rey decided he looked too dull to be worth any conversational effort. He picked up his beer and strolled out to the empty verandah where he settled himself in a swing-chair. Down below was the swimming-pool and there was the dark-haired girl he had noticed the night before. She was using the spring-board with unselfconscious expertise—her lithe body knifing neatly in the air before slicing smoothly into the water. And, immediately, she was again up on the board and repeating the performance. Time and again she did it.

She was, he believed, one of the Russians. They were usually suspicious, the Russians, about any overtures of friendship. He'd found that in the past. But she looked attractive enough to make it worth trying. At least, she might relieve the boredom of the day . . .

He watched the bounce of her bottom, jaunty under the clinging wetness of her black costume, as she re-treated toward the line of changing-huts. And by the time he had finished another cigarette she was walking towards the steps of the verandah, now wearing a simple floral dress, with her wet costume and towel over her arm.

He took the initiative as she was about to pass him. "You dive very well," he said.

"I'm sorry?"

"I've been watching you diving and I was just saying that you dive very well."

His French accent gave Barbra an automatic feeling of dislike. It stirred too many unpleasant memories from the tragic jumble of her childhood. The frightened families being evicted from their homes—the humilia-tion of the de-lousing stations . . . these and other pain-ful pictures from the past were suddenly vivid again because of the inflections in his voice. She smothered her thoughts and smiled. "You are most kind," she said. "One is a little out of practice . . ."

He got up. "May I offer you a drink?"

"Well . . ." There was uncertainty in her manner.

"Please." He indicated a chair. "I would be grateful for your company."

"Then thank you. A gin please, with tonic."

He pressed a bell-button and a boy appeared from the bar to take the order.

"Cigarette?"

She smiled again and shook her head. "I used to," she said. "But my brother was always saying they are bad for one."

She produced a small silver box from her handbag

and sniffed a discreet smidgeon of snuff. "Now I use this instead. My brother says it is better."

"And you always do what your brother says?"

"My brother Jan is very wise," she said. "He is a good man."

The drinks arrived, her gin and his new beer.

"Are you here on holiday?" she asked.

"No, I work here. I'm a pilot."

"That must be a very interesting job." She emptied the tonic into her glass. "Which airline?"

"No airline," he said. "I'm President Amin's personal pilot."

He was pleased but not surprised by her sudden and obvious interest. His job, he felt, gave him a certain social distinction. It usually impressed women . . .

"Beautiful plane, he's got," he added. "A Cessna Citation."

"Yes, that is a beautiful aeroplane," agreed Barbra. "And it handles well too."

Now it was his turn to be surprised. Girls never knew anything about aircraft performance. "You *know* the Cessna Citation?"

"Twin turbofan," said Barbra. "Cruising speed is 348 knots at 25,400 feet . . ."

She started laughing. "I'm sorry, I'm not being fair," she said. "I should have told you that I'm an aircraft specialist. That's why I'm here in Uganda."

"Well I'll be damned. You look much too pretty to have a technical brain."

"One doesn't have to have warts on one's nose to have a technical brain," said Barbra. "And in my country, in Poland, women can do all sorts of work."

"Well, well, isn't that just marvellous," he said. "So we've got something else in common."

"Something else? What was the other thing?"

He was thinking of how she'd looked in that tight wet costume. "Swimming," he said quickly. "I, too, am very fond of swimming."

The tall German he had seen in the bar walked past them, carrying a towel and trunks, and went down the steps of the verandah.

"Perhaps we might have dinner together," suggested Pierre. "We could talk about swimming and about aeroplanes."

"Thank you," said Barbra. "That I would enjoy."

Theodor made a great noise as he hit the water. It really was a terrible dive. And, watching him from the verandah, they could see he wasn't much of a swimmer either.

* * *

Theodor did not hear the news of the reported invasion. He was still dressing after his swim when the first details came over Radio Uganda:

"Heavy concentrations of foreign troops, aided by white mercenaries and infiltrators inside Uganda, have crossed the border from Tanzania at Mutukula. They have been met with determined resistance and fierce fighting is taking place. Reports are now being received of many casualties.

"It appears that the invaders are intending to try battering their way north through Masaka in the hope of eventually capturing Kampala.

"But President Idi Amin Dada orders that the loyal people of Uganda are not to feel fear. They are to remain confident that this wicked and unprovoked aggression, inspired by the powers of white imperialism, is doomed to certain failure.

"His Excellency has assumed personal responsibility for supervising the defeat of these invasion forces and troops of the Simba Battalion at Mbarara . . ."

A state of emergency was being declared. People were being told to keep off the streets. And security chief Moloro was ordering that all foreigners—except those with "special clearance"—were to be arrested immediately "for their own protection."

But Theodor knew nothing of these swift and dramatic developments. He finished dressing and went to his room. Then, after draping his damp costume over a rail in his bathroom, he tidied his hair before wandering casually down to the foyer of the hotel.

The foyer was curiously empty. There was only the doorman, at attention as usual, by the main entrance, and the clerk behind the reception desk. The clerk seemed apprehensive, shuffling papers as if trying to look busy and carefully averting his eyes from Theodor.

Then they came rushing in from the street. There were seven of them—three with sub-machine guns and others with automatic pistols—all in their early twenties. Their leader was dressed in a blue tee-shirt, flared trousers, suede shoes and a baseball cap. He was also wearing dark glasses. Similar gear was being worn by the others, except for the man at the rear. He had a buttoned-up shirt with no tie and a blue serge suit a couple of sizes too small. On his head was a trilby with a long yellow feather sticking from its band.

Theodor had never seen them before but he knew immediately who they were. He had heard so much about them. They were members of Uganda's Special Branch—the official terror men who had authority to torture or murder without motive.

Theodor stared at them, astonished. It was impossible that the plot had been discovered already . . . wasn't it?

They surrounded him, prodding him with their guns, and he could smell the alcohol on their breath.

"Passport!" shouted the leader.

Theodor took his passport from an inside pocket and gave it to him. The leader passed it, without a word, to the man behind him. His eyes, all the time, were on Theodor's face. "Passport!" he shouted again.

"But you've got it," said Theodor. "Look—there it is—I just gave it to you."

The man with the trilby had now come to the front

and he stabbed Theodor, harder than before, with the barrel of his machine-gun. And Theodor saw the man with the passport starting to rip it to pieces.

"No passport?" shouted the leader.

"But he's . . ."

"Quiet!" The man's breath was quite foul. "It is an offence for a foreigner to be in Uganda without a passport. You are a foreigner and you have no passport. You are under arrest."

They marched him out of the hotel. The street, normally so full of life, was deserted except for a pie-bald dog lethargically scratching at fleas.

A small and battered car was at the curbside and, with a great deal of angry shouting, they forced him into it. Two of them took the front seats. One was at the back next to Theodor and a fourth sat on Theodor's knees. This fourth man kept a pistol pressed into Theodor's left ear.

"Where are you taking me?" asked Theodor.

The man twisted the gun, tearing the skin in Theodor's ear. "No questions," he said. "You are a spy. A white imperialist spy."

The driver stayed in the car when they reached the Central Police Station and the others hustled Theodor into the building. There were no formalities in the reception area. No explanations or papers to be signed. It seemed as if he was expected. They gun-marched him past the long counter, where armed soldiers and policemen were slouching and watching with casual curiosity, and turned him along a corridor to the right. No words were spoken now. One of his captors was leading the way and the other two were jabbing him along from behind with the snouts of their guns. A man on a stool jumped up quickly when he noticed them coming and unlocked the gate of stout iron bars which caged the end of the corridor. Through the gate, which clanged heavily behind them, and down a flight of concrete steps to a second gate. That was also banged shut after they had been let through. And now he was hit by the staleness and the stench of the overcrowded prison.

They had arrived in a semi-basement reception area, gloomily lit by two naked and inadequate bulbs. More light—a little but not nearly enough—drained through a small window, covered with a metal grille, which was high in a corner wall.

A warder with a pistol holstered at his hip, who had been writing at a small desk, stood as they approached.

"This man is very dangerous," he was told. "He is a spy—an enemy of Uganda."

The warder nodded. "Over here, then," he said.

Off this reception area, beyond still more heavy gates, were two blocks of dungeons. The block on the left was for ordinary prisoners—for petty thieves, drunks and prostitutes. This was the temporary-residents section and the occupants, once they had served their fixed sentences, would normally be released. Each cell in this block, where men and women were herded in together, had the luxury of its own primitive lavatory of a hole in the floor. The block on the right, far darker and filthier, was for the special prisoners—those labelled "enemies of Uganda." Many of these prisoners would never know freedom again. Some, like the fisherman from Kahirimbi, would have their skulls smashed by a mallet. Others, perhaps the less lucky, would die more slowly and agonisingly. There were no holes in the floors of these cells. At the far end of the block was a small row of evil-smelling lavatories to which the special prisoners were taken under armed escort twice a day. Those who were forced to relieve themselves outside the ordained lavatory times had to use the floors of their cells.

Theodor was taken to the right and pushed into the fourth cell along. There was no furniture in it. No chair, no bed, not even a blanket. It measured about nine feet by seven feet and there were already three men in it—two black Ugandans, squatting with their backs to a wall, who stared uninterestedly at him with expressionless eyes, and a young white man, flat on his stomach with his face on the urine-stained concrete, who was trembling violently as if with a fever.

The Special Branch men had now gone, presumably to hunt fresh victims. "Later you will be interrogated," said the warder as he locked the door.

The young man's eyes were closed. "What's the matter with him?" asked Theodor. "Is he ill?"

The black men ignored him. Perhaps they could not understand. Perhaps they were too obsessed with their own miseries and fears. They were waiting for death, and such things as a trembling white man were not important.

And, quite illogically, Theodor was suddenly remembering another condemned man, a man whose death he had once watched. He could almost see that man as he had been then, frightened and weeping and standing so ludicrously on that little stool . . . pantomiming for the amusement of his tormentors before being shot.

And then, remembering how that small and pathetic body had tumbled to the floor, he felt fear for himself. He had not told the German authorities he was going to Uganda so they would make no representations on his behalf. They did not know and so they could not try to intercede. The only people who even knew he was in the country were those involved with Sanity International, and they could never speak out.

He could disappear, just disappear for ever, and there would be no-one outside to ask questions.

He also wondered about the mission. Would Lajeba, perhaps not knowing of his arrest, be busily going ahead with his part of the operation? That could be disastrous because—

His thoughts were interrupted by the trembling man who was now trying to speak. "Tell them . . . for God's sake tell them . . ." The man, who had an American accent, was having difficulty in forcing out the words.

Theodor knelt by him. "Tell them what?" he asked.

The man raised his head a couple of inches from the floor and tried to look at Theodor but he was too weak. "They'll die. The guards . . . the whole goddamned lot . . . they'll die if they don't listen . . ."

Theodor put an arm gently around his shoulders. "I'm listening," he said. "Tell me."

"I've tried to tell them . . . but they don't listen . . . they don't understand . . ."

"Tell me," repeated Theodor.

"I'm ill . . . very ill." Theodor had to crouch closer to catch the words. "I'm a medical student and I know there's more than one thing wrong with me . . ."

"Go on," encouraged Theodor.

"And one of those things is infectious hepatitis. You hear me? Infectious hepatitis! If they don't get me out of here soon the whole goddamned prison will be down with it . . ."

Theodor got up. "Guard!" he shouted. "Guard—quickly!"

*   *   *

PIERRE REY: Many people confuse me with Marcel. We are twins. Not identical, but still strikingly similar in appearance. We have the same slight build, the same sallow complexion. His black-olive eyes, intense and intelligent, could almost be my eyes. And his hair, like mine, is prematurely receding.

But our similarities are physical—and nothing more. It would be hard to find another pair of brothers so very different in character.

He is generous and kindly and undemanding. He is, in fact, a fool. It's not really his fault—he just has to live with the nature issued to him.

Me . . . well, I'm a selfish bastard. It's as simple as that and I make no secret about it. This is a stinking sod-you sort of world and you've got to grab what you can.

Money . . . power . . . women , . . no matter what

it is. If you want it—snatch it. And if that means doing someone the dirt—well, that's how it has to be.

When we were boys it was just the same. I was always pulling some real strokes and always managing to wriggle my way out of them. Somehow it was usually Marcel—poor, puzzled Marcel—who finished up with the blame.

We lived at Uzerche in the region of Corrèze and our father was a schoolmaster. He was very hot on discipline. I remember the time when I nicked the apples from the orchard. That was about 1958, when we were twelve. Well, I'd nicked apples often enough before but this time it was different. Calmin the farmer damn near caught me—only he wasn't too sure if it was me or Marcel. Anyway, he came round to our place in one hell of a rage.

Naturally, both of us—Marcel and myself—denied having touched his apples. Then my father went searching through the house, just as I'd guessed he'd do, and he found the apples in Marcel's duffle-bag. God! Did he beat him that day! And he warned him about the wickedness of telling lies . . .

Then, later, there was Yvette. She came from a good family, a wealthy and respectable family, but she had this habit of mislaying her pants.

At some time or other, I would guess, just about every boy in Uzerche went with Yvette. Except, of course, for Marcel. It wasn't his style to go with girls, not in that way. He wasn't queer or anything but it was just that he had these funny ideas about saving it up for marriage.

It was me, however, who got Yvette pregnant. At least, she said it was me and I did have this gut feeling that she was probably telling the truth.

Then, would you believe, she wanted me to marry her! It was too ridiculous for words—but I couldn't make her see it that way. We argued about it, on and off, for the best part of a week and then we worked out a compromise.

I'd just finished my training as a pilot and I was aiming to go off and see the world. But she obviously ought to get married—it was, in the circumstances, the done thing in a place like Uzerche—and it seemed best to keep things in the family. She, we agreed, would marry Marcel.

He had almost completed his studies in archaeology at the time and Yvette admitted that he would make a solid and reliable father. After all, we had to consider what was best for our child . . .

Of course, we did not mention our decision to Marcel. It seemed best not to.

Even Yvette, with all her experience, found it difficult to seduce my dear, innocent brother. He clung to his virginity like a bear to its honey. But—inevitably, considering how she worked at it—he finally offered it in surrender . . .

Then, later, all she had to do was tell him she was going to have a baby. And, naturally, he immediately offered to marry her. My father, I remember, was very angry with him. No member of the Rey family had ever before had to marry in such circumstances. It was a disgrace . . .

She had a miscarriage, not long after the wedding, and I was really sorry about that. I hadn't fathered any other children, not as far as I knew, and it would have been interesting to watch the growing-up of my son.

So that's the way it has been with Marcel and me. All through out lives.

And now comes this! Of all the people in the world, why should this have to happen to me? I've always been so healthy, so active and full of life. It's so bloody unfair.

Still, at times like this it's good to have a brother like Marcel—a brother prepared to make such a sacrifice.

If it comes off, and it's got to come off. I'll owe my life to Marcel. Quite a thought, that, isn't it?

I'm damned sure I wouldn't jump to make the same sacrifice, not if things were the other way around. It would be hypocritical of me to say otherwise for I've never pretended to be anything but what I am.

I put myself first, no matter what the circumstances. And I don't see that calls for any apology.

* * *

Cherif the Moroccan, like all the others picked by Stanton, was extremely efficient. He had organised transport for the abduction of Marcel and Yvette Rey —across sea and land—and had also prepared the hiding-place in the Rif mountains. He knew his reward would be high and he had worked conscientiously. Now he was on his way to meet the Englishman called Carter.

It was late evening and Carter, alone on the deck of the tramp-steamer, knew that night would soon suddenly envelop them in its shroud of black velvet. He scanned the distant water impatiently but saw nothing.

He glanced at his watch. Any time now. Still he waited. He did not want to give the Reys their injections too soon.

They were below, locked in their cabins, as they had been all the voyage from Istanbul, and they could have no concept of where they were or where they were going. It was better that way. They would have to know eventually, of course, but for the moment it was better.

Weaver had gone for a shave. One man was at the wheel and, with little to do at that time, the other four members of the crew were drinking and playing cards.

Still nothing to be seen. Carter frowned. They were now at the rendezvous—eight miles north of Sebta, which squats on the Moroccan coast east of Malabata Cape and the city of Tangier. It was a good place, just outside Sebta, to disembark a secret human cargo.

Suddenly, on the horizon, he saw it. At first it was no more than a match-head and he wasn't completely sure that it was really there. Then there could be no doubt. The motor-launch, superb and graceful, was hurtling towards them at an amazing speed.

"Cut engines! They're here!" shouted Carter.

Almost immediately, it seemed, Weaver was at his side, a towel in his hand and traces of lather still on his face. "Shall I give them their jabs now?" he asked.

"No hold on a moment," said Carter. "I'll come and give you a hand."

The steamer, which had been moving so very slowly before, was now merely riding the slight swell. And, just as darkness was falling, Cherif was securing the launch alongside and clambering aboard.

"Cherif?"

He nodded and gave a huge friendly grin.

"I'm Carter and this is Weaver."

They all shook hands. "But don't forget that you never mention those names, not when our guests are with us," added Carter. "Our names—as far as they are concerned—are Richards and Black."

"And, the same way, nobody calls me Cherif, eh?"

"What do you want to be called?"

"Oh . . . anything. Tommy, perhaps." Another gigantic grin. "Tommy is a good English name, yes?"

"Okay, Tommy," said Weaver. "We'll go down and fetch them. You wait here."

Marcel cowered away when he saw the hypodermic in Weaver's hand. "Why are you doing all this?" His voice was quavery. "Where are you taking me?"

"You won't be harmed," said Weaver. "That's a promise. Just take it easy and you won't be harmed."

"No, get away—get away from me—"

Carter grabbed him and held him tight while Weaver slid the needle into his arm. They carried him unconscious to the deck and Cherif helped transfer him to the launch.

It was the same sort of pattern with Yvette. Except, Carter thought, that she was much more fun to hold.

They had no lights on, not wishing to attract any attention, as they headed towards the coastline they could not see. Cherif's navigation was impeccable and, well before the Reys had come out of their stupor, the launch was nudging up a lonely and unwatched beach. Beyond the narrow strip of sand was a clump of trees which Cherif pointed out to Carter. "That's where I've got the truck," he said. "It's just off the road."

They laid Marcel and Yvette on the sand while they dragged the launch partially clear of the water. Then, while Cherif roped it securely to a retaining peg, Weaver and Carter carried them towards the trees.

Weaver was to travel in the back of the covered truck with the Reys. Carter locked him in and hurried to join Cherif in the front. "Now where?" he asked.

"Now we go for a long ride," said Cherif, starting the engine. "To a town called Chaouen. It's about a hundred kilometres from here and I have a place there that no-one will find."

Carter lit a cigarette. "Well, Tommy, I just hope you know what you're doing. Personally, I'd have stayed clear of any town.

"Is that an English cigarette?" asked Cherif. "English cigarettes are my favourites. And American cigarettes— they are my favourites as well."

Carter handed him the lighted cigarette and fixed another for himself. "There can be too many people in towns. Too many inquisitive people . . ."

"You are right," said Cherif. "And in Chaouen everybody is inquisitive."

"Well, then, surely . . ."

"But we won't exactly be in the town." Cherif inhaled deeply and grunted with satisfaction. "Sometimes I think English cigarettes are better than American cigarettes. English cigarettes, I think, are my best favourites."

"But if you know they're inquisitive . . ."

"I know because I was born in the town. I know everything about the town. That is why I know about the caves."

They were now turning on to a main road towards the south.

"What caves?"

"Where you will be living. In the Rif mountains. The big caves." He chuckled. "There is so much room in those caves. A rich man could keep all his camels in them."

"But supposing somebody comes up there," said Carter. "That could wreck everything."

"Nobody will come," replied Cherif confidently. "That I know. People in Chaouen, and in the places around, are afraid of the caves. There are old superstitions. They say the caves are . . . what is the word?"

"Haunted?"

"Yes, that is the word. Haunted. I am always forgetting that word."

They were moving at speed now along a deserted highway. Cherif threw his finished cigarette out of the window. "That was very good," he said. "You have many English cigarettes?"

Carter handed him the packet with seven still in it. "But, obviously, you're not afraid."

Cherif chuckled again. "The money from Mr. Stanton," he said. "It is enough to stop me being superstitious."

"It might even be enough for you to start buying your own cigarettes," said Carter.

And Cherif laughed uproariously. He liked to show that he could appreciate a joke.

*   *   *

They had been in the caves for nearly two hours and Marcel, alone in the innermost one, was trying to assess the situation. He had no idea which country, or even which continent, they were in. And he had no idea why he and Yvette were being held prisoner in this manner.

A paraffin lantern gave this inner cave a reassuring light and enabled him to study the huge store of tinned provisions. It looked as if, for some reason, these men were prepared for a long seige.

Weaver stooped his way in through the low entrance of rock separating the middle cave from the inner one and then stretched to his full height. Marcel decided to try yet again. "Mr. Black, please . . . you've got to tell me . . . is this for money? I'm not a rich man and if it's a ransom you want . . ."

Cherif had driven down to the medina in Chaouen to collect three of his cousins. Two were to help keep sentinel in the three inter-communicating caves. The third would eventually return the truck—borrowed for a fee but for an unspecified purpose—to yet another cousin living in Ketama. Cherif had many cousins. He also believed that business should be kept within the family.

Carter, glad of the chance to relax after the travelling, was sprawled on a rock outside the outer cave—enjoying the tranquillity and the cleanness of the mountain night air. Yvette was seated near him, watching the glow of his cigarette in the darkness.

"You're very casual," she said conversationally. "Aren't you worried I might run away? In this darkness you'd never find me."

"Go ahead. Run," he replied. "You'll break your pretty neck. There are sheer drops all around us and I promise you will find them—especially in this darkness."

"And how long is this idiotic performance going on? You and the Australian . . . you can't watch both of us indefinitely, you know. Not day and night. You've only got three eyes between you."

Somewhere, down in an unseen valley, a giant frog was grumbling rhythmically. And a chorus of tiny tree-frogs was replying in soprano.

"There'll be eyes to spare," said Carter. "Tommy . . . the lad who drove us here . . . he'll be back soon with some of his mates."

"And this Tommy . . . what's he? Tunisian?"

Carter saw no reason why, at this stage, he should not tell her.

"That, I take it sweetheart, is a subtle way of asking which bloody country you're in. Well, you don't need to be subtle about it. You're in Morocco. Half-way up a mountain in Morocco and, apart from our little gang, there's no-one for miles. So don't go getting girly ideas about screaming for help."

"You're a very reassuring man, Mr. Richards." Her voice was remarkably cool. "That really is your name, I suppose—Richards?"

"My friends call me Dick."

"Short, presumably, for Richard. Mr. Richard Richards. Hardly original, is it, Dickie?"

Carter finished his cigarette and its redness traced a high arc as he flipped it. "Forget the bloody label. Call me what the hell you like. Richards . . . Dick . . . a name's a name. It's not important."

"I'll settle for Dick. Now tell me, Dickie dear, what is all this about? Who are you? And what exactly do you do?"

Her last question reminded him of a girl in London. A girl called Magyar. He'd put that question—well, one damned like it—to her and, at the time, he'd been almost shocked by the reply. Now he couldn't help laughing over the memory. Magyar . . . his first married woman . . .

"Did I say something funny?"

"No—just an old, old private joke," he said. "Something I'd almost forgotten."

It was obvious he was not going to answer her questions and there was a long silence. "Could I ask you for a cigarette?" she said eventually.

"Why not?" He got up and moved towards her. "Everyone else seems to be bumming mine today."

He placed a cigarette between her lips and she steadied his hand with her own as he held a match. And, after he had thrown the match away, he explored her face with the tips of his fingers. She made no move to resist or draw away when his hands wandered down her neck and he began gently squeezing her breasts. She was conscious of her nipples swelling in response.

"Please," she said quietly. "My husband . . ." But there was no conviction or authority in her voice.

She dropped the cigarette as he kissed her. One hand went around his neck and the other crept, like a small and stealthy animal, into his groin.

CHAPTER 3

There was jubilation in the voice of the Radio Uganda news-reader as he announced the catastrophic defeat which had been inflicted on the invasion forces from Tanzania. They had been forced to flee in terrified disarray—abandoning their dead and dying inside the fringes of Uganda.

This, the news-reader explained, was yet another great personal triumph for His Excellency President Idi Amin Dada for it was His Excellency who—again demonstrating his genius and immense courage—had personally secured the victory.

In a special statement from his Command Post near the border His Excellency had advised all the nations of the world—particularly the sinful white regimes of Rhodesia and South Africa—to think deeply on this display of the invulnerability of the military might of Uganda. Once again it had been proved that no army was a match for Uganda under the leadership of President Amin.

Only minor casualties had been suffered by the brave men of the loyal Ugandan forces.

Lajeba, in the course of his official duties, often had to visit the Presidential Palace. There were so many conferences to attend, so many documents to present for the signature of the President. Amin used his palatial home as the control-centre of the country, regarding Government House as a subsidiary office-block for typists and routine chores.

Now, with the tension of the invasion over—and with

both the President and Moloro away from the capital—security was far more relaxed than usual at the Palace. Lajeba noticed that almost as soon as he entered. The sentries, normally so alert and suspicious, were very much at ease and some of them were smoking and giggling over private jokes. The President's personal servants, with whom he had cultivated an easy, bantering relationship, were obviously grateful for having a couple of undemanding days.

The country was being encouraged to celebrate its victory and the Palace, as if infected by the almost-carnival atmosphere outside, was in a holiday mood.

This delighted Lajeba for this was the day when he had to achieve the trickiest and most hazardous of the tasks set for him by Stanton.

In his briefcase, together with the bundles of official papers, was a hard-backed book measuring five inches by seven inches.

At least, it looked like a book when it was closed. Its heart had been neatly cut away, leaving just the outside edges of the pages, and in the oblong cavity was a small but lethal bomb. He handled the case with immaculate care for he was very conscious of the two wires inside the book. It would take very little pressure to force them together and then there would be an explosion severe enough to shatter any room.

Any servant watching Lajeba that morning would have suspected he was mad. His actions, most of them, seemed so irrational. But there was no-one to watch. He had made certain of that by his timing—not intending to move into action, wearing his new black gloves, until exactly 11:30. That was when a taped message from the President, still in the battle zone, was to be transmitted on Radio Uganda. And at that time, for ten respectful minutes, everyone in the Palace would be listening to a radio. The network of domestic corridors, leading to the private rooms of Amin and his most trusted men, would be deserted . . .

At exactly 11:32 a.m. Lajeba entered Moloro's bedroom. He acted fast—taking a bottle of whisky, three-quarters full, from the dressing-table and a leather-bound copy of the Koran from the small cupboard by the side of the bed. Then, again making certain he was not being observed, he slipped from the room and at 11:36 he was in Amin's private bedroom. Only two people ever went into that room—Amin and his personal eunuch body-servant. It was forbidden even to Amin's wives. When Amin decided to see them he visited them and then, invariably, returned to the sacred privacy of this room.

Lajeba hesitated, just for a moment, and then gently placed the book-bomb under the centre of the mattress. He smoothed the covers so that they appeared undisturbed.

In an open corner cabinet there was, as he had known there would be, a selection of full bottles of alcohol. Not one had been opened. He took a bottle of whisky and replaced it with the partially-drunk one from Moloro's room. On a bedside table was a copy of the Koran, identical to the one he was now holding in his gloved hands. This was not surprising. These Korans, as he had seen from the documents at Government House, were part of a bulk purchase. They were rarely read, for religion played no major role in the world of Idi Amin. They were, however, standard issue in the Palace, rather like pieces of unwanted but obligatory furniture. He swapped the books and, after peeping to make certain the corridor was still empty, he left the room. He glanced at his watch. Eleven-thirty-nine. The worst part was now over but he was taking too long. There was only one minute before the end of the President's broadcast . . .

Back in Moloro's room. Amin's Koran, wiped of any finger-prints, went where Moloro's Koran had been. Amin's whisky, also wiped on Lajeba's sleeve, went on Moloro's dressing-table.

It was over. And now, for the first time, he realised just how much he was sweating and trembling.

"That was a wonderful speech by the President," said the guard commander at the main gate. "An inspiration of a speech."

"Truly inspiring," agreed Lajeba as he got into his car. The full text, he knew, would soon be in the newspapers. He had to read it as soon as possible.

Back in his office at Government House he waited. The telephone call from Theodor should be coming through almost any time now.

He nibbled skin from around his left thumb-nail and spat tiny bits of it on to the carpet, rehearsing in his mind what he would have to do when the call came.

A secretary brought him coffee in a blue-and-white beaker. He was pleased to notice that the beaker was not chipped. So many of them were.

"There weren't any messages for me, were there?" he asked. "While I was out—there weren't any messages?"

"I wasn't here all the time, Mr. Lajeba, but Belinda would have told me if there had been. She didn't mention any."

He was tempted to tell her to send Belinda in but, realising that might make him seem too anxious, he felt it better to wait. "Right, thank you."

The girl smiled politely and left. He nibbled away another bit of skin. Theodor should have called by this time. He was long overdue. Stanton had been most specific about the need for meticulous timing . . .

The coffee was not good. Not bad but not good. As he started to sip it, he had a sudden frightening thought. That order which had been given by Moloro . . . the one about foreigners being arrested for their own protection . . . it had seemed so routine that, at the time, he had not absorbed its full portent . . .

Of course—that just had to be the explanation! Theodor, somewhere, was being held captive.

The more he thought about it the more obvious it seemed. Now he was plunged into an agony of anxiety and indecision. It was too late, far too late, to try removing the bomb for the President was already on his way back to Kampala and the Palace security would again be at its strictest. It was possible, even, that Moloro had travelled ahead and was already there.

When the bomb went off—as it must unless there was some miraculous intervention—Amin would unquestionably be killed. Bits of him would be spattered all over the walls and the ceiling. The Muzimu were no match for the sophisticated device which was inside that mutilated book.

It was imperative that did not happen, for that style of killing would shatter everything they had planned.

Perhaps he or the girl Barbra could manage to play the role designed for Theodor. But he was rejecting that idea almost as soon as it came. He knew it would be quite hopeless. Amin would never accept either of them in the necessary position of trust. The link with Hitler was vital . . .

So everything had to depend on Theodor. But was Theodor even still alive? Lajeba knew of the ferocity of the Special Branch squads . . .

There, in the quietness of his office, he stared at the desk and groped desperately for some answer. He could find none. The operation, it seemed, was slithering towards disaster.

*　　*　　*

KARL THEODOR: Our house in Saarland, like those clamped on either side of it, is old and gaunt and ugly. It is a tired house. Number forty-seven in an ash-grey street. Outside the front the pavement is cracked and it smells of garbage and stale urine. At the back there is a patch of neglected earth where the worms make mounds and the weeds grow proud. And beyond are the sourly-smoking chimneys of the houses behind. They are the same, those houses. In the next street and the street after that. All just the same. And over it all, permanently hangs the great cloud of sulphurous filth. It comes from the marshalling yards to the north and from the blast-furnaces to the west. They make pig-iron there, in those furnaces, and most of the men work in them. My father is Auguste Ernst Theodor. He has two brothers who work in the blast-furnaces but he is a shoe-maker. He is also a member of the Party and he teaches me, his only son, to be proud of the Party.

May, 1933. Hochbauer is the mathematics master and we are frightened of him. He is wizened and elderly and has viperous little eyes. He does not give punishments. He has never been known to give punishments. But there is a malignancy about Hochbauer and us boys, all aged about twelve, are frightened of him.

He is not due in the classroom for ten minutes and some of us are playing rough games. Boys are cruel and in our games there is nearly always a victim. Bieber is the favourite victim because he is gangly and walks around with his mouth slack open. He is the victim because he wears pebble glasses that make him look goofy. He is not stupid but he looks stupid and he always gets angry. So Bieber is the victim.

We are harassing Bieber, ruffling his hair and jostling him with our shoulders and, without him knowing, I manage to take the pen from the breast-pocket of his shirt. He is proud of that pen, is Bieber, and so I am going to hide it. Later we are all going to enjoy watching him while he searches for it. We have done it before. We have done it with his compasses and the pump from his bicycle. It is fun watching Bieber search for he gets so deliciously angry . . .

Hochbauer arrives and we are all at our desks. And then, as the lesson starts, Bieber acts unfairly out of character. He raises his hand for permission to speak and he tells Hochbauer that his pen has been taken. Yes, he is sure he had it when he entered the classroom. No, he is certain it is not just mislaid.

*"Then we have a thief in the class," says Hochbauer.
Thief! I feel as if the word is being branded on me.
"I want the thief to own up," says Hochbauer.
Nothing happens.
"So," says Hochbauer. "The thief is also a coward."
It is getting worse. Much worse. Now, because of
Hochbauer's cruelty, I am trapped.
"The boy who has stolen this pen will be punished,"
says Hochbauer. "He will be punished, not by me but
by his own conscience. He will live with the guilty
knowledge that he is a thief and a coward."
I manage, unseen, to secret the pen inside my right
sock. It is safer there.
"However, I am prepared to ease that punishment
for him," says Hochbauer. "I cannot stop him being a
coward, for cowards are born, but I can give him the
chance to stop being a thief. When this lesson is over
we will all leave the room as usual and tomorrow I
will expect to find Bieber's pen on my desk. I will then
return it to Bieber and I will ask no questions."
Now we are out of the classroom and I want to slip
back but I am frightened that Hochbauer has laid a
trap. I am frightened of finding him there waiting for
me. So I take the pen home and I dare not tell my
family that I am now a thief and a coward. And I hide
it in a drawer under my clean vests.
Weeks pass. I am in secret torment over the pen. We
have laughed in the past, me and my friends, about the
things we have taken from Bieber. But this time I cannot tell them for this time it is different. It is not a
joke now and I am a thief.
Hochbauer is away from school. They say he is ill.
I am relieved for I feel that perhaps Hochbauer suspects
me. Every night, just before I go to bed, I look at the
pen. I want to throw it away, to get rid of it for ever,
but I feel that would be a wicked thing to do so I push
it back under the vests. And sometimes I worry that
my mother might discover it . . .*

Then comes the news that Hochbauer is dead. He died of pneumonia and pleurisy. And for me the nights get worse. I lie in my bed in the darkness and I remember the words of Hochbauer. I remember him talking about the punishment of conscience. The pen is so near me in the room and, in my dread, I build a fantasy around Hochbauer. Now he is dead and the secrets of life have been opened to him and he knows that I am the coward and the thief. Fantasy becomes reality. I can feel his accusing presence. He is wizened as he was in life and his viper eyes are baleful with reproach . . .

I am cold in the darkness and I sweat with adolescent dread. I know I must give the pen back to Bieber. Hochbauer will never leave me in peace until I give the pen back. My mind writhes around the dilemma. There is no-one in whom I can confide, for to confide would be to confess. And the crime has now grown too big for confession.

Hochbauer, now long in his grave, continues to haunt my nights. Then I have the plan. It is born in desperation, this plan, but I am excited because I know it will work. And Hochbauer will know, at last, that I am not really a thief.

I get a sharp tool from my father's workshop and, very carefully, I gouge Bieber's name on the shaft of the pen. I take the pen, again hidden inside my sock, back to the school and, now that is out of my room, I am already starting to feel relieved.

In the corridor by the physics laboratory there is a bench. There is no-one else in the corridor so I put the pen on the bench and I hurry away.

Later I see the puzzlement on Bieber's face. Some-one has found his pen, the one he lost so long ago, and has returned it to him. It is obvious it belonged to him because his name is scratched on it. And Bieber is baffled because he knows he has never put his name on the pen.

"Isn't it the most curious thing?" says Bieber. But nobody pays him much attention. He looks so goofy

and it is obvious that he has got it all wrong. And Hochbauer no longer reproaches me. I am no longer a thief. Just a coward.

June, 1939. My papers come for military service. I am glad because now I can escape from the blast-foundry. My father's eldest brother, Heinz Theodor, is a foreman and he got me the job. He means well but I hate the clattering din and the heat. I feel suffocated and trapped in the blast-foundry. So I am glad when my papers come.

My girl is called Sybille and she lives with her drunken mother on the other side of the marshalling yards. She weeps when I tell her I am going to the garrison at Stuttgart because she loves me and Stuttgart is another world. I tell her I will soon be back on leave and that she will be proud of me in my fine Wehrmacht uniform. She asks me to think of her always and not to go with strange girls in Stuttgart. All the soldiers go with strange girls in places like Stuttgart, she says, and I wonder how she can know of such things. I promise her I will not be like the other soldiers. I will think of her. All the time I will think of her. And she clings to me and she cries again. One day, perhaps, I will marry Sybille and take her away from her drunken mother. She has blonde hair and she is very beautiful.

In Stuttgart, like all the other young soldiers, I go with the strange girls. I am frightened that I might catch something nasty but still I go with them. And I write to Sybille often to tell her I am thinking only of her.

Poland. Poland in September. We are splendid men in the Panzer Divisions and we are invincible. Our officers have told us we are invincible and so we know we are. Ignacy Moscicki, the President of Poland, has made a stupid broadcast. He has told his people: "The entire Polish nation with the blessing of God in a just and holy cause, united with the army, will go shoulder to shoulder into battle and to final victory." And the people are so trusting that they believe him. To final victory! What do they hope to do? Break our splendid cannons with their pitch-forks? Rip apart our tanks with their bare hands? It is sad and pathetic. We have to kill them. It is necessary in war.

They cling to the words of Ignacy Moscicki and the campaign goes on. Corpses. Dead corpses and living corpses. Men who can still swear and bleed and complain and kill but who are already corpses. They have died, degree by degree, without knowing they have died. They have been killed by the killings all around them. By the killings and the atrocities.

We reach a museum in the district called Kepno and the lieutenant decides that we have fought valiantly and so we deserve a bit of sport. He forces the curator to go through the museum smashing the show-cases and the treasured exhibits with a brick. The curator is a meek man who weeps as he does his destruction. This is the sport. Then the lieutenant makes the curator stand on a stool in the middle of the rubble with his right arm up in salute. Seven times he makes the curator shout "Heil Hitler!" And then he shoots him dead.

I see my friend Otto crush the head of a small child with the butt of his rifle. He is a good man, Otto, but he crushes the child's head. He does it because he is no longer the Otto I went whoring with in Stuttgart. He is still intact and he still functions but he is dead.

Now I fear things being done in our name. They are not right. And I am ashamed because I know I would still carry out any order, no matter how awful it might seem, because I would be frightened to disobey. Hochbauer the mathematics master knew about me. He suspected it when he was alive and he knew it when he was in his grave. I was twelve at the Hochbauer time, at the time of the pen, and I was a coward then. Now I am eighteen and I am still a coward.

The village is called Torzeniec and it is in the district

known as Ostrzeszow. We are told that this is a bad village and that its people are bad people. An example has to be made of them. All the men in the village stand by a wall in a line and every second one along is to be shot. I am not picked for the execution squad and I am grateful. It seems wrong, even in a village as bad as Torzeniec, to shoot defenseless men as they stand against a wall.

"Set fire to all the houses!" shouts the lieutenant later. "Set fire to all the farm buildings!"

We have our orders. We are to shoot everyone— men, women and children—who comes out of the blazing buildings. For this is still the bad village of Torzeniec and if the flames do not destroy them then our bullets must. My gun is aimed at a young woman who is running with a baby in her arms. Her clothing is torn and filthy but she looks a bit like Sybille. The same sort of blonde hair, the same neat body. I tilt the barrel just a little high and I squeeze the trigger. I keep firing towards the sky and my comrades are too busy to notice that I am not killing anyone.

The earth of the flaming village is now drenched with blood and the blonde woman with the baby has disappeared into the smoke, and I silently pray for her safety.

I cannot obey my orders but I am frightened my officers will realise I am not obeying my orders. My conscience is clawing at me but I am a coward.

August, 1966. Now it is all long behind me—the war and Saarland and the shabby house where my family was bombed to death. The blast-foundry is still there but, after leaving the army, I have not gone back to it. And now I live in Munich. I am the tallest policeman in Munich and my superiors regard me as a good police-man. Two months ago my drunken mother-in-law, Sybille's mother, died with cirrhosis of the liver. No-one was really sorry when she died because no-one really loved my drunken mother-in-law.

There are times when I go drinking. I drink to lose the memories of Poland and of France. I drink to drown the shame of being a coward. And Sybille drinks to keep me company.

November, 1970. Some people can drink and then not drink. They can take it or leave it. I can and so can both my sons but Sybille is not like us for Sybille cannot stop drinking. She is an alcoholic. Now she is drinking more and more. The house is untidy, the dishes are unwashed. She falls down the stairs and she sleeps where she falls. She hides bottles in the attic and behind the food in the cupboards. She hides them under the beds and in the bicycle shed. We have rows about money, for we cannot afford such drinking on the pay of a policeman, and the doctor warns her that she will also die because of drink. But Sybille goes on drinking and no-one can stop her.

May, 1974. Things are different now, for Sybille no longer drinks. She has been getting help—help from the doctor and from some men and women who have been through the same troubles—and she has not been drinking for nearly a year.

She says strange things. She says she has been told not to take even one little drink because that would turn her back into what she once was and she is frightened of that happening. This is crazy talk for I can see she is cured. She was an alcoholic, that I can understand. But that was in the past . . . and she is no longer an alcoholic. Why cannot she have just one drink? One small drink. Where is the harm in that?

She does not have that drink because she knows this gives her a power over me—it makes me feel guilty. I can see how her mind is working. She feels she is superior to me because she does not drink. She never says anything but she never needs to say anything for, particularly when I am getting drunk, I can see it in her eyes. She is patronising me! I challenge her about it. I quarrel with her over it. But always she denies it.

"Prosit!" *I want her to have a glass as well but she refuses. She is my wife and she refuses to drink with me! So I shout at her and I ask her again and she starts to get angry. She tells me that I am a fool and then, quite suddenly, she snatches the glass from my hand and drinks it at one gulp. For a moment she looks oddly defiant but now everything is all right. I can see she is enjoying the drink. She is no longer angry. She has a second glass and then a third. We have a very jolly evening.*

Sybille is still sleeping when I wake in the morning. She looks so at peace that I do not disturb her. I make my own breakfast and I leave for duty.

It is early evening and I am preparing to go home when I get the telephone message. And, at first, I cannot believe it.

The doctor, later, is soothingly considerate. Sybille, he says, must have been drinking all day, right from the time she got up. Then she was dreadfully sick—and she choked to death on her vomit.

"You must understand that there is no such thing as a cured alcoholic," he says. "An alcoholic is an alcoholic for life. It is a sickness which can never be shaken off. It can only be arrested in its progression if the sufferer keeps strictly away from drink. Your late wife, unfortunately, gave way to temptation . . ."

My friends are also sympathetic and I cannot bring myself to tell them the truth. Sybille did not die because of a sickness or because of an inherited weakness. She did not die because she gave way to temptation. Sybille died because I, in my evil stupidity, forced her to drink. I killed my wife, just as surely as if I had taken a knife or an axe to her. I cannot tell anyone of these things for they are too disgraceful and I am a coward.

And now there is, within me, a great emptiness. I think back over the years of my life and I wish I could unravel them and start again. I stop drinking, of course, because somehow it seems disloyal to Sybille's memory to go on drinking. And I yearn, so very deeply, to do something of real value to help make up for all the wasted years. But there is nothing now that can be done.

Evil never dies. It flourishes and withers—only to flourish again. I have watched it happen. I have, in the days of my innocence, helped it to happen. And I am constantly reminded of that fact by the stories in the newspapers about this dictator in Uganda who has such a great admiration for Adolph Hitler. I remember how there was a time, when I was young and believed my shoe-maker father, when I also admired Hitler. No, that is the wrong word. I worshipped Hitler. Then came the disillusionment and the disgust . . .

He is a bad man, this Amin. A dangerous man.

I talk about him and about my feelings—which are disjointed and jumbled—to Gottschalk. He works in government intelligence and he is an old and trusted friend. He seems to understand, to appreciate how I need to do something. It is he, Gottschalk, who introduces me to the American called Stanton.

*   *   *

They were spread out through the three caves. In the first, the one leading directly on to the face of the mountain, Marcel was hunched and brooding, being watched by Weaver and Cherif's two sentry cousins.

"All those things I found in Turkey." He was wearing his melancholy like a black cloak. "All those things . . . all wasted and thrown away . . ." He hugged his arms around his knees and stared miserably at the earth. A tiny beetle was climbing jauntily up the treacherous slope of his right toe-cap. He did not notice it. "The curator of the museum would have been so delighted . . ."

"He still will be," said Weaver. "At least, he will be if the stuff's all you crack it up to be." He stretched and expanded his chest in a huge yawn. "It's safe, every bit of it, so quit the worrying."

Marcel spotted the beetle as it was beginning to step-ladder up the symmetrical ridges of his laces. He flicked it with his index finger and it landed, legs working agitatedly in panic, on its back in the dust. "Then where is it?" he asked.

"Listen pal, I've told you before about that. Questions . . . questions . . . always bloody questions."

He saw the look on Marcel's face and relented. "Aw, all right—I'll tell you this much. When all this is over, and it shouldn't be long now, you and your wife will be sent safely on your way. You'll never know who the hell we are or why we've been holding you but that won't matter. You'll be safe and you'll be free to go home. Then you can start living your ordinary lives all over again, just the way you like it . . ."

Marcel leaned forward to help the beetle on to its stomach. It hurried to hide gratefully behind a pebble. "But the pieces from the dig," he said. "You say they're safe."

"A week after you get home a big, fat parcel will arrive. You won't know who sent it or from where. But, inside, you'll find everything. I guarantee that. Every grubby little relic—it'll be there intact. That's a promise, so now you can drop the bloody subject."

He had to bend a little as he went through to the central cave where Yvette was helping Cherif prepare a meal. He nodded at her and jerked his thumb behind him. "Your husband's got some news for you," he said.

Carter, relaxing in the inner cave, looked up as Weaver entered. "All well?"

"No, all is not bloody well," said Weaver. "Do me a favour, will you, and quit screwing Yvette."

"What the hell do you mean?"

"Surely you understand?" Weaver was picking his words slowly and with heavy sarcasm. "Screwing. You understand screwing, don't you. Or is there some fancy British word for it?"

Carter started getting up. "I know what screwing means."

"Then you don't need an explanation. No diagrams or anything. So just cut it out."

Carter was now standing to face him, his eyes aggressively defiant. "Why?"

"Because this is a job, that's why. And because I'm not having you or anyone else getting emotionally involved."

Carter looked bemused for a moment and then he started to laugh. "Let me tell you something, chum," he said. "When it comes to screwing, as you choose to call it, emotions have sod-all to do with it. It's purely a mechanical thing—understand? Nothing to do with the emotions at all, and I should know. I've screwed my way around the world—on duty and off duty. I've screwed—that really is an ugly word, by the way, but let's stick with it since you picked it—I've screwed women of just about every nationality under the sun. It's a hobby, chum, a hobby, so don't start prattling at me about emotional involvements."

"This one is married," said Weaver.

"So? Most of them are."

"I've got a thing, Carter, about adultery. It gives me a tight feeling right here in the chest. I don't like it, so just cool it."

"Piss off," said Carter. "Anyway, I'm not at all sure Yvette would want me to. She doesn't get much from him, you know, and she's an enthusiastic lady."

"I don't care if she's Madame Bloody Nympho!" Weaver suddenly realised he was shouting and he lowered his voice. "I don't care," he repeated. "Just keep away from her."

"Well, well, well," said Carter. "Fancy me, of all people, getting stuck with a moralising Aussie." He began to mock in a drawling Coon voice. "So, Mr. Preacher Man, you think adultery is a sin, eh?" He stepped forward, his face now close to Weaver's. "We can kidnap them, kill them, do what the hell we like—

as long as we don't have it off with their wives. Is that what you're saying?"

Weaver moved back, away from him, and wiped his hand down the left of his face from his temple to his chin. "It was adultery that cost me my eye," he said.

"I've often wanted to ask you about that. What was it? Some angry husband with a hat-pin?"

Weaver restrained an urge to smash a fist into his sneering face. "Mind your own fucking business," he said.

*   *   *

The guard did not know whether to believe Theodor. Prisoners, particularly those in the special block, tried so many tricks. But he was also frightened that, if there was any truth in what Theodor was saying, he might be considered responsible.

He sought the advice of his superior who, in his turn, found himself in the same quandary. Eventually, after much discussion, they decided it would be safest to get a doctor to examine the sick American and, because they knew the medical man there would be immediately available, they called the British High Commission.

The British doctor—small, short-sighted and disapprovingly precise—knelt on the dirty floor of the cell and vigorously shook his bald and narrow head. "He can't possibly stay here," he said. "Every moment he is here he is a danger to all the others." He looked up sternly at the guard. "Move, man, move." It was almost as if he was at medical school, addressing some singularly stupid student. "Get on to your superiors immediately. Tell them what I've said and that it is imperative for them to make arrangements. Go on—shift yourself."

The guard was flustered for a moment and then he hurriedly retreated towards his reception area. The two black prisoners in the cell were still vacant in their own worlds of emptiness and Theodor seized the moment to crouch by the doctor and whisper urgently to him. "There is a government official called Lajeba," he said. "Edson Lajeba."

The doctor shook his head testily. He did not know what Theodor wanted but, whatever it was, he was not going to get involved.

"He is an important man and he works in Government House," persisted Theodor.

The doctor appeared not to have heard. Theodor glanced anxiously through the bars to make sure the guard was out of ear-shot. "I have a vital message that I must get to this Lajeba. You must give it to him for me."

"I'm here to tend this man," said the doctor. "That's all I'm here for and that's all I'm doing. No messages."

"Call Lajeba at Government House and tell him that you have seen me—Karl Theodor—here in prison."

"No messages," repeated the doctor crossly. "I'm not here for messages."

Theodor looked anxiously again. Still no sign of the guard. "Remember my name—Theodor. Tell Lajeba that I know of a plot to kill President Amin."

The doctor looked at him with distaste. "What plot?"

Theodor knew his time was short. He could hear the guard returning. "If you fail to tell Lajeba, President Amin will die today," he whispered. "I can save him. If he does die, you will be responsible."

"Rubbish," said the doctor.

"It will be because you have refused to help save him."

"Tell the guard," said the doctor. "Here he is, coming now. Things like that—they're not my business. Tell the guard."

"Please believe me," begged Theodor. "The guards cannot be trusted. Just make one telephone call—that's all I ask. Tell Edson Lajeba that Theodor is here in prison and that he knows of a plot to assassinate the President."

"I don't know," said the doctor. "It's not my job."

* * *

"Give me his name again," said Lajeba into the telephone.

"Theodor," said the English doctor. "A German. Odd sort of chap. A bit barmy, if you ask me."

"And what exactly did he say?"

"Just what I've told you."

"Thank you," said Lajeba.

"I'm not supposed to carry messages, you understand," said the doctor petulantly. "It's not my job."

"I know and I'm grateful to you," said Lajeba. "Thank you again." He replaced the receiver.

The coffee-making secretary and the girl called Belinda stared in surprise as he ran from his office and out of Government House. His hand was wedged to the horn-button, blasting other traffic aside, as he sped to the Presidential Palace. There he summoned the guard commander at the main guard. "I must talk to the President the moment he returns," he said. "Before he does anything or sees anyone. This is a matter of the highest importance to the State."

The guard commander was impressed. "I'll do my best," he said.

"Do better than that," said Lajeba.

Forty minutes later he was in a private room with Amin.

"And how does this Theodor know you or even know of you?" asked Amin.

Lajeba was standing to attention while Amin lolled comfortably on a thickly-padded leather couch.

"We first met by chance in London, Mr. President," said Lajeba. "At a diplomatic party."

"But he is not a diplomat."

"No, Mr. President, but he has many friends who are diplomats. Men who, like him, are still fine and dedicated Nazis. They have to be discreet about their feelings these days, of course, but in their hearts they are still loyal to the old values. It was one of them, now in the West German diplomatic service, who invited him to the party."

Amin was immediately interested by the reference to Nazism. "So he was a Hitler man, eh?"

Lajeba did not hesitate. This was part of the script he had rehearsed many times in his mind. "No man, Mr. President, could be more dedicated to the ideals of Herr Adolph Hitler than Karl Theodor. I know because we talked about it at great length. He told me, in fact, that he had a tremendous admiration for you because, in so many magnificent ways, you reminded him of Herr Hitler."

Lajeba wondered for a moment if he was not going too far too fast but, reassured by the beam of child-like pleasure on Amin's face, he went on: "He said, Mr. President, that he considered you and Herr Hitler as the two greatest and most inspiring leaders of this century."

Amin nodded approvingly. "Hitler," he agreed, "was a fine man. How well did this Theodor know him?"

"Perhaps as well as any man, Mr. President. He had the honour of being picked as one of the Fuhrer's senior personal body-guards. There was one occasion— and this I did not hear from Theodor for he is too modest—when he saved the life of his Fuhrer. He risked his own life to do so for there was a lunatic with a gun . . ."

And, as he recounted the graphic story of the mad-man who never was—and of how the heroic Theodor had wrestled with him—he could see that Stanton's assessment was absolutely correct.

Workmen, even at that moment, were completing the shrine to Hitler in the heart of Kampala—the shrine where, Amin had decreed, the people of Uganda would eventually kneel in homage. Now . . . to have a man who had been chosen by Hitler as his own personal protector . . . a man who had actually saved the life of the Fuhrer . . . this was more than a mere matter of prestige. This had to be the work of destiny. Amin, in this matter, could almost feel the tangible and comforting embrace of the Muzimu.

Amin was trying to restrain the excitement welling within himself, trying not to betray his growing conviction that this man, this Theodor, had been sent to Uganda by a benevolent Higher Power. He spoke curtly: "And about this so-called plot. You have no more details?"

Lajeba shook his head. "None, Mr. President," he said. "Of course, I did press the doctor, but he'd told me all he knew."

"Then go to this Theodor and find exactly what he knows," ordered Amin. "If he is talking sense, I may feel the need to interrogate him personally."

Lajeba, with his authorisation signed by the President, was escorted briskly through the Central Police Station. Through the iron gate at the end of the corridor, down the concrete steps, and through the second gate. He was shown into a tiny white-washed interview-room—without any window—just off the reception area. Two hard chairs faced each other across a scrubbed table. There was no other furniture.

"Get the German," said his escort to the guard.

Both of them returned with Theodor. "Leave us," said Lajeba. "I want to talk to him alone."

They went out, closing the door behind them, and Lajeba motioned Theodor to take the chair opposite him.

"The doctor?" asked Theodor.

Lajeba nodded.

"Thank God."

"You fit?"

Theodor grimaced. "Fit enough."

"Good," said Lajeba. "The book is on the shelf. Everything is as planned."

"But how the devil do I . . .?"

"It's all fixed," said Lajeba.

"And what's all this about an invasion? I heard men talking in the next cell. Something about an invasion from Tanzania."

"There was no invasion," said Lajeba quietly. "Always when people start getting restive—because of shortages of food or whatever—the President arranges a side-show, a distraction, for them. It takes their minds off other things. It also makes it possible for him to show what a hero he is—going into the thick of the battle and repulsing the enemy—"

"But these men were saying that some of Amin's own troops were killed. They'd heard it on the radio."

"Blood is often shed in Uganda," said Lajeba. "There are always men the President needs to dispose of— military men, usually, who are starting to get ambitious. It suits the President for the people to believe that these men stayed loyal to him, that they died loyal—fighting the invading enemies of Uganda . . ."

"And what about people like me?" asked Theodor. "Would we be killed?"

"Not unless the Special Branch boys particularly disliked your face," said Lajeba. "Then they might kill you, just for the amusement. But normally you'd have been kept in prison for a few days and then you'd have been kicked out of the country. Deported as an undesirable alien. There'd be talk of you being a spy who'd been treated with mercy . . . it would make useful propaganda."

"So these men—these soldiers—they were really murdered by Amin?"

Lajeba's front teeth made a tiny click as they met through a piece of finger-nail skin. "Actually they were murdered by Moloro and his team. And that was a stroke of good fortune for us. Moloro actually went there—but not until a few hours after the President. So the story fits exactly. And, something more, I've discovered that Moloro actually was in the bar at the Metropolitan just before your arrest. It's a perfect jigsaw."

"So what do we do now?"

Lajeba stood and moved towards the door. "I have to telephone the President and then, I think, you will be released," he said. "After that we follow the plan exactly."

Theodor nodded his understanding. "Right," he said.

Lajeba opened the door. "Guard!"

The guard and the escort hurried in. "Stay with this man. I will be back directly."

He returned within a few minutes. "Come," he said to Theodor. "You have an appointment with President Amin."

CHAPTER 4

Theodor was on his knees. He had to crane his head back at an uncomfortable angle to see Amin who, with Moloro a couple of paces behind him, was seated on a velvet-covered dais.

Amin had never forgotten the arrogant fools of British officers who, when he was a sergeant, had made him jump in response to their ridiculous commands. Now he liked being able to look down on white men. He liked seeing them crouched before him in servility. It emphasized his success and it reinforced his feelings of superiority. There would come a time, he was confident, when the whole white world would kneel at the feet of Idi Amin Dada.

This big German was a special man, a man who had once actually saved the life of Hitler, but his skin was still disgusting and white. So, until the President wished it otherwise, he would remain on his knees.

"Why did you not tell this to the men who arrested you or to the guards in the prison?" demanded Amin suspiciously. "To wait, as you did, shows some lack of concern."

"It was because of my concern, my fear and concern for you, that I could not speak to those people, Mr. President," said Theodor. "I am a policeman, a man who once had the supreme honour of personally serving the illustrious leader of the Third Reich. And as a policeman, Mr. President, I know the dangers of trusting people. Your life, sir, is far too precious for me to take the gamble of confiding in strangers."

Amin grunted noncommittally but the reply seemed to satisfy him. "The man Lajeba—you felt you could trust him?"

Theodor had a painful crick in his neck and his knee-caps were aching. "In London, when I met him, Mr. President, I realised that he was the most devoted and loyal of your subjects. A policeman, a good policeman, has an instinct in these matters."

Another grunt from Amin. "Stand up if you want to," he said. "You say you didn't see these two men you heard talking in the hotel."

Theodor had a pin-rash in his left leg. He gratefully rippled the muscles as he got up. "I regret, Mr. President . . . they were behind the greenery partition. And that, of course, is why they did not see me."

"So you said. But are you certain you didn't hear any name mentioned? Any name at all?

Theodor was conscious of Moloro watching him with cold and impassive eyes. "Well . . ."

"Why are you hesitating?" demanded Amin fiercely. "There is something you are not telling me?"

Theodor looked down at his toe-caps, seemingly reluctant to reply.

"Is there?" shouted Amin.

"I don't know, Mr. President," said Theodor evasively. "I just don't know for sure . . ."

"You are a policeman!" said Amin. "You should know for sure!"

Theodor took a deep breath and then, as if reaching a sudden decision, he said: "It is my training as a policeman, Mr. President, that makes me hesitate. Adolph Hitler, when I served him, was a hard man but he was a fair man. I believe from all I have heard, Mr. President, that you are a man in the same mould. You are fearless and you are fair. So you—if I may respectfully say so, sir—would not wish me to be unfair. You would not wish me to perhaps incriminate an innocent man because I spoke too soon, because I spoke before I could be sure."

He paused, hoping that the flattery would have the right effect, but Amin merely waited for him to continue.

"There was a name," said Theodor. "But it meant nothing to me and it was difficult for me to catch because—forgive me—I am not familiar with African names. I wrote down the name as I thought I heard it—"

"Where?" interrupted Amin. "Where did you write it?"

"In my diary. In the back page of my diary."

"And where is that diary now?"

"I imagine it is still at the hotel, Mr. President. In the pocket of my jacket."

Amin glanced back at Moloro. "Get it brought to me," he said.

Moloro was already moving towards the door when Theodor, aware that this was a crucial moment, begged Amin to stop him. "All my instincts as a policeman—and I do have a great deal of experience, Mr. President—my instincts, they tell me it would be better for that name, if I heard it correctly, to be left as the final bit of confirmatory evidence."

Moloro was hovering uncertainly now, anxious to obey his master but no longer sure whether or not he was to go. He did not have to hover for long.

"Do as I say!" shouted Amin. "Send for it immediately!"

"No!" Even Theodor was surprised by the ring of determination in his own voice.

"Please, Mr. President . . . please, before he goes . . . hear what I have to say. For it is your life and the future of this great country that is at stake . . ."

Again Moloro looked at Amin for confirmation of the order but Amin signalled him back. Amin scowled at Theodor. "Well?"

"I do not know this man," said Theodor indicating Moloro, "or those who serve under him. I am merely a visitor, a stranger in your land. But my experience in Germany, particularly my experience under the great Adolph Hitler, has taught me much. It has taught me that no man is above suspicion. The messenger that this man will send—how can we be certain that it will not be *his* name in the diary? Do we go out of our way to warn possible enemies? Do we alert them? or do we stalk them and trap them with stealth? Only the three of us here in this room know there is a name written in that diary. Even Lajeba does not know for I did not tell him."

He addressed himself to Moloro. "You have, I take it, a finger-print expert here?"

"His name is Aswa," said Moloro. "He studied in Russia. He is trusted and highly-qualified."

"He may be highly-qualified but no-one is to be trusted," said Theodor. "Absolutely no-one."

He was now starting to feel in control of the situation and he turned again to Amin. "If I could presume to suggest, Mr. President . . ."

"I am listening," said Amin cautiously.

"I would suggest that to start with the three of us— with this man Aswa—should make a careful study of your room. Of course, I do not know what we may find but that, I would urge you, should be our first step."

Amin rubbed his chin thoughtfully and reflected for a few moments. He recognised that here before him was no ordinary man. Here was a man who had once saved the life of Adolph Hitler. "And then?" he asked.

"And then," said Theodor, "we will be in a better position to decide the next move."

Amin looked at Moloro, obviously inviting an opinion. Moloro was resentful of his role being taken over by this tall German but he could think of no valid objection. He nodded sullenly. "I agree," he said.

Amin clapped his hands once, loudly and decisively. "We will go now," he said.

The four of them—Amin, Theodor, Moloro and Aswa the finger-print man—went quietly to the bedroom and closed the door.

"Mind the bed," warned Theodor. "Do not touch the bed."

Moloro saw the chance to snipe and, more important, to start regaining his authority. "It seems to me that you are an unusual and perhaps even a cowardly policeman," he said with brutal politeness.

The reference to cowardice hit Theodor particularly hard, but he showed no reaction.

"We must touch the bed, with the President safely in some other place, of course," went on Moloro. "We must do that in order to defuse the bomb—if there is any bomb here."

"Then you do it," said Theodor quickly. "We'll all get well out of the way and you stay here and do it."

Moloro was now less confident and Theodor pressed harder. "Have you heard of something called a trembler? They use them a lot in places like Northern Ireland. The slightest touch, with one of those tremblers, can set off an explosion. Booby traps—that's what they use them in. But you're the one with the courage so perhaps we should leave it to you. You try defusing it . . . and I'll help scrape you off the wall afterwards . . ."

Amin intervened. "What do you wish to do?" he said to Theodor.

Moloro, now squashed back into a subservient role, was glowering self-consciously but there was nothing he could say.

"Well, Mr. President, it's more a question of what I'd like you to do—if you don't mind me suggesting it, that is. This bed, I am certain, has been tampered with and it is possible that the intruder might have touched or even moved something else in the room."

Amin seemed dubious. "Your logic—it sounds strange to me."

"The minds of wicked men work in strange ways, Mr. President. I have seen it often before. When I was employed by the Fuhrer there was an occasion when—"

"There! That whisky bottle!" said Amin. "It was full. I know it was full . . ."

"Check that bottle for prints," said Theodor to Aswa. "Handle it carefully, now."

Amin was intrigued but still puzzled. This German seemed to have his priorities wrong. It was the bomb surely, if there really was one, that should be dealt with first. And, anyway, even if there were finger-prints on the bottle, how could they possibly know who had put them there?

Theodor explained that the bomb could do no harm as long as it was not touched—but that every moment wasted before an identity was established was allowing more escape time to the would-be assassin. He also explained that the intruder must have been someone who knew the Palace, someone who could move around the corridors without raising undue suspicion. A list of such people would have to be prepared. Servants . . . clerical staff . . . officers . . . Every one of them, discreetly, would have to have his finger-prints checked.

His reputation as the man who had once saved the life of Hitler was still dazzling Amin.

"And, as an essential matter of routine," he added, "it will be necessary for Aswa here to take sample prints from the three of us as well."

"You are suggesting that I might plant a bomb in my own bed?" Amin was now openly incredulous. "I choose women for my bed—not bombs."

"Forgive me, Mr. President, for not making myself clear," said Theodor hurriedly. "Such prints—and it would be essential to have Aswa's prints as well—would be used purely for purposes of elimination."

"Very well." Amin sighed and shrugged as if determined to humour a demanding child. "Moloro—you first."

It was the first time he had addressed Moloro by name and Theodor appeared startled. "Moloro? *You* are Moloro?"

"That is my name. Why?"

"Oh nothing . . . nothing at all. I just didn't realise you were Moloro."

"Is it of some significance to you?" demanded Moloro.

"No . . . that was very rude of me. Please accept my apologies."

Aswa took impressions of their prints. And, as he was about to leave with his equipment and the whisky bottle, Theodor stopped him for final instructions. "This, you will realise, is a top-secret affair. Not a word must be mentioned to anyone. Men will be sent to you, one at a time, and you will not tell them why. And, in view of the seriousness of the matter, it will be best for you to present your findings personally to the President." He glanced at Amin for approval and Amin nodded curtly. "You will not report to me or even to Moloro . . ." He paused and apologised again to Moloro. "You do appreciate that, in a situation such as this, it is right that the President has first priority on all the facts."

Moloro did not appreciate it. He merely appreciated the fact that his job as security chief was being completely usurped and he could see no easy way to regain it. This German would have to be discredited and deported. Some opportunity, some excuse, would have to be manufactured. "Of course, I appreciate that entirely," he said.

Then Amin noticed the Koran on the bedside table. "That book has been moved," he said. "I am certain it is not in its usual position."

"Take the book as well," said Theodor to Aswa.

Now for the trickiest part. The actual detonation.

Theodor sent for a huge reel of fine rope and a small metal weight. He threw one end of the rope through the window, to where Moloro was waiting in the gardens, and he ordered Moloro to tie it to one of the lower boughs of a tree two hundred feet from the wall of the building.

He watched Moloro carefully, waiting until he was satisfied that the rope was securely tethered. Then, with Amin a fascinated observer, he fed the other end of the rope down through the neck of the funnel light-shade immediately over the bed. It dangled limply between the shade and the bulb and Theodor tested it carefully to make certain that, right along its length, there was no slack. He went to the window and tried to pull the rope from the tree. It remained taut. And now it was taut, with none to spare, all the way up to the lampshade. "Please, Mr. President, would you now stand back." With infinite care he tied the metal weight to the bit of rope sticking out from the bottom of the shade. It hung there, a square spider on a thread, barely eighteen inches above the covers of the bed. "Now it is time for us to join Moloro," he said.

They reached the tree where, by now, a small group had gathered. Theodor, as if this was part of some time-honoured ceremonial, bowed with stiff formality as he handed a knife to Amin. "It was intended, Mr. President, that the bomb should be set off by you," he said.

Amin smiled. "I dislike disappointing people," he said. "It is not in my nature."

There was no sound from the spectators as Amin approached the rope. They could sense that something dramatic was about to happen but they could not imagine what that something could be. The rope was so puzzling, stretched like a fisherman's line with the tree as its mighty catch. And Theodor remembered the words of Stanton. "Make it flashy and spectacular." That's what Stanton had said on the boat at the Isle of Wight. He'd said it before the others had arrived and he'd kept emphasizing it. "Make it flamboyant and as outrageous as you can. They're like children." That's what Stanton had said. "They're like children and they can be swayed by a showy performance." This, thought Theodor, should be sensational enough to impress any of them. Particularly Amin.

Amin raised his hand, glanced around to make sure every-one was watching, and then severed the rope with a great slashing motion. There was a sharp pinging noise as the released section jerked upwards and snaked towards the Palace. And, almost instantaneously, Amin's window belched a great sheet of orange flame. The roar came a split second later and, with it, the apologetically skinny plumes of black smoke. A shred of white bedding fluttered to the ground like a singed snowflake. A tatter of multi-coloured curtain clung drunkenly to the outer sill before slithering to the flower-bed below. And the frail columns of smoke went on climbing from the devastation in soldierly, pencil-straight lines.

The stunned silence was broken by the raucous bassoon of a tetchily-disturbed hornbill in the distant trees and Amin beamed at the spectators as if he had just accomplished some amazing feat. "You see!" he said. He put an arm around Theodor and hugged him affectionately. "This is a good man," he said. "This one was sent by the Muzimu."

Two hours later Theodor was again summoned to see Amin who, as at their first meeting, was seated on the dais. No-one else was present and this time he made it clear that he did not expect Theodor to kneel.

"Aswa has reported," said Amin. "You are a shrewd man. I have a feeling you will not be surprised by what he has discovered."

A knock at the door and a messenger entered. He handed Amin a diary which Theodor recognised and then left. Amin did not open the diary.

"You were surprised, however, in my room when

you first heard the name Moloro. Why were you surprised then?"

"I believe, Mr. President, that you now know the reason."

"Yes, Aswa has reported," said Amin again. "He did find finger-prints on the Koran and on the bottle. They are the finger-prints of Moloro."

Theodor shuffled uncomfortably. "I was fairly sure," he admitted. "But I was not absolutely sure. A policeman needs to be absolutely sure. That, Mr. President—and I beg you to forgive me—was why I took the liberty of organising that charade in your room."

"My new room is even more beautiful," said Amin. He opened the diary. "Which page?"

"The back page," said Theodor.

Amin turned to it. "You have spelt Moloro wrong," he said.

"You may remember that I did explain, Mr. President, how—unfortunately—I am not familiar with all African names." Theodor was being earnest and apologetic. "I wrote what I thought I heard . . . but I was anxious not to throw blame on to an innocent man."

"Very commendable," said Amin. "I can understand why Adolph Hitler regarded you with such esteem. I, too, like a man to have a feeling for justice and a sense of compassion. Compassion is a very important quality. I always recommend it to my enemies."

He stood and walked from the dais. "Now I must arrange the death of Moloro."

"What will you do with him, Mr. President?" Theodor, despite himself, was now feeling just a little sorry for Moloro. "Will you have him shot?"

The question, for some reason, seemed to strike Amin as amusing. His shoulders heaved with laughter and tears came to his eyes. "No, no, no . . . that would be barbarous," he said happily. "Bullets are for ordinary people. A man as important as Moloro—he deserves something far more original."

He began pacing backwards and forwards, his brow furrowed in concentration as he mused over the possibilities. "There is an English poet called Gilbert Sullivan," he said eventually. "He is not a good poet but he has wise thoughts. In one of his pieces of poetry—and it is now so popular that the English have even set it to music—he describes what should be done with an evil man. He says, in this poem, that the punishment should fit the crime."

"The *Mikado*," said Theodor. "That's in the *Mikado*."

Amin shrugged aside this superfluous bit of information. "It is poor poetry but good wisdom," he said. "This punishment will have to be very special. I must consult with Ogwal."

* * *

Major Anthanasius Ogwal, Uganda's Head of State Ceremonials, liked to boast that he had the most imaginatively original mind in East Africa. The boast was probably a fair one. He was also a sadist of the highest calibre.

The banquet of the severed head—with Brindeba's sightless eyes and the accusing turn-table of death—had been spawned in the ingenuity of Anthanasius Ogwal.

The obscene techniques of forcing men and women to eat themselves, stuffing their throats with roasted flesh hacked from their own legs and buttocks—these sprang from the inspiration of Ogwal.

And his body was almost as grotesquely distorted as his mind. People might say he was fat—as they might say Everest is high or the Atlantic is wide—but "fat" was a snivelling inadequacy of a word for a man like Ogwal. He was not fat. He was gorbellied and gargantuan, monstrous and megalithic.

Theodor, seeing him approach for the first time, was

boggling at the sight. All those sweaty pouches of boot-brown lard! Every ungainly, waddling step sent them pitching and wallowing like the humps and troughs of some greasy ocean. Every breath seemed an uncertain triumph of determination over obesity.

And, when Ogwal reached him, Theodor found there was something more . . .

Ogwal had a disconcerting habit of talking in a solid grey monotone—and giggling in a high castrated pitch—without ever moving his sausage lips.

Words and sounds seemed to float out of him as if they were merely passing through without ever having been formed by him. He also gave off a most unpleasant smell.

"Something special, something very special—that is what is wanted by our most excellent and exalted President," said Ogwal. "So something special it will certainly be."

He released a brief burst of that idiot cackle. It reminded Theodor of the high notes of an off-key xylophone.

"You, I am told, are Theodor," said Ogwal.

Theodor stood back a pace to avoid the odour. "That's quite right," he said.

"Of course it is," said Ogwal. "You are Theodor and you will help me, Theodor. You and me together—we will provide something so wonderfully special for our President."

He linked an arm through Theodor's. "Come," he said. "There are arrangements to be made."

* * *

A little to the north of Kampala, just off the Luwero road, was a magnificent natural amphitheatre—a gigantic soup-bowl of stunted grass and barren earth set in the broad-backed hills. Many men had died there, some alone and some in massacres, and it was known as the Pit of Death.

Now, in the fragile light of early evening, hordes of spectators were swarming across the slopes around the arena. They had travelled from the city and its surrounding villages, from Entebbe and Jinja, from places as far away as Kayonza and Nabusanke. They had come because they had been promised the most exciting and elaborate public execution ever seen in Uganda —the execution of Frederic Kasozi Moloro.

Moloro's death was indeed to be special. Special and spectacular. He was to be the nation's sacrificial offering to the Muzimu. They had intervened yet again to save the life of the President. And Moloro's ceremonial death was to symbolise the joyous gratitude of the people of Uganda.

Major Anthanasius Ogwal, with a huge entourage of immediate subordinates, had been busily making arrangements for two days. Streams of monotone orders had constantly flowed from his motionless lips and he had been permanently sweating and waddling—forever devising and delegating—as he had switched his attention from the Pit to the Palace and back again to the Pit. His eyes had been fired with evil delight as he had supervised the plans for the carpenters and the jugglers, the dancers and the fire-eaters. And he had not been able to refrain from giggling hideously as he had discussed the technicalities with the helicopter pilot.

"Excellent," he had kept saying. "Our most exalted President will be highly pleased."

And now, with the great moment approaching, he was confident that the President would be more than just pleased. This time he, Ogwal, was truly demonstrating the depths of his genius . . .

He stood on the planks of the high canopy-shaded grandstand which had been built for the Presidential party at the southern side of the arena and studied the crowds with satisfaction.

Ugandan flags were rippling from the tops of four specially-erected masts and, halfway up each mast, was a powerful spotlight. These lights were not to be switched on until the appropriate moment. Down below, hunched around the rim of the bowl, were the teams of drummers in their gay traditional costumes. At the signal of command they would start with one stark and solitary beat. Just one superbly-synchronised beat. It would reverberate around the packed slopes of the Pit, lingering in the stillness of the evening air. Then, after a dramatically-calculated pause, it would be followed by a second lonely beat. And then slowly, almost imperceptibly at first, the pauses between the beats would become briefer. The tempo would quicken. And eventually the frenzy of the hundred drums would be flooding the Pit with its blood-rousing vibrance.

He glanced to his left where Amin was seated with his senior officials. Theodor and Lajeba were in the small group standing immediately behind the President. And at the back of the grandstand were the trestle-tables from which the servants would be serving food and iced drinks.

Amin nodded. Ogwal raised his pistol and fired into the air. That signal brought the first great boom from the drums . . .

Soon the arena was filled with the entertainers. Warriors with shields and assegais fought savage but bloodless battles, battles which had been choreographed by tradition and time. And after the warriors came the others. The men who ate flames, their leader leaping and somersaulting on the back of a massively-grave elephant, were followed by the jugglers . . . and the bare-breasted maiden dancers . . .

Amin was eating imported strawberries and nodding his satisfaction and the crowds were roaring their approval.

And now, in the descending dusk, there was a great silence of expectancy.

Only one sound could be heard—the spluttering drone of an approaching helicopter. Its twin rotors brought it whirring over the lip of the eastern hill and it hovered for a while over the centre of the arena which—apart from four waiting attendants—was now empty. Then the spotlights came on together and, in their cross-beams, the crowds could see that something was dangling on a hawser from the helicopter. They could not make out quite what the thing was but it looked strangely like a starched and cumbersome bell-tent. Gently, with the lights following it, the thing was winched to the ground where the four attendants tugged away the canvas covering.

There were gasps of amazement when they could see what was now revealed. The glare of the lights showed a small bed. And, imprisoned on it under a birdcage contraption, was the unmistakable figure of Moloro. He appeared to be drunk or in some drugged stupor for he was climbing clumsily to his feet, clutching to the bars for support, before falling heavily backwards on to the mattress. Again he tried and again, like a circus buffoon, he tumbled.

Amin joined in the laughter. "My head of security seems to be over-fond of his bed," he commented. "It is not fitting that he should be lying there at this time of day. It does not show the dedication to duty which I have the right to expect from such a man."

"It is not good at all, Mr. Exalted President," agreed Ogwal seriously. "It is, I must presume to suggest, a sign of great disrespect."

"Then perhaps we ought to get him up," said Amin.

"Immediately, Mr. Exalted President."

Ogwal again fired his pistol into the air and an unseen trumpeter began to play the reedy notes of a military reveille. Now it was completely dark, with only the pool of artificial light around Moloro. And as the final note from the trumpet was fading the helicopter pilot adjusted his winch and the bed-cage began to rise.

Higher it went, and still higher. The hawser and the helicopter could no longer be seen. The illuminated bed appeared to be magically suspended in the night sky. And there it hung for two or three minutes before the first of the fireworks . . .

It all began with the white, green and orange of the Catherine Wheels spinning on the boards at the foot and the head of the bed. Then came the cascades of Golden Rain . . . the beauty of the Silver Fountains . . . the glorious red-tailed rockets which banged off rainbow trails . . .

They exploded and soared and tumbled through the night sky in a riot of colours and the crowds gaped in breathless wonder at the sight. And finally, startlingly, came the great finale. The whole bed exploded and disintegrated in a great burst of fire and tiny bits of debris were flung into the distant blackness . . .

The helicopter moved away over the eastern hill and soon its sound was lost.

Amin pushed another strawberry into his mouth and turned to Theodor. "It seems that my security chief has just died," he said conversationally. "I need a replacement. You will take the position?"

"It would be a high honour, Mr. President."

"Then it is settled," said Amin. "Your things will be moved into the Palace tonight."

"Thank you, Mr. President, I am most grateful. There is, however, just one thing . . ."

"Yes?"

"As I am a German, a stranger in your land, it would be most helpful for me to have an assistant who knows the ways of Uganda, an assistant I can trust."

"Lajeba?"

"He would be ideal, Mr. President."

"Then he is your assistant," said Amin. "He will also live in the Palace."

And then came the beginning of the tropical storm. Thunder came rolling low over the hills like the deep-throated roars of some huge and hungry animal. The sky curdled and became theatrically vivid with lightning and the first fat globs of rain spilled over the crowds. Soon it was a torrential downpour, drowning the roads and churning the tracks into red porridge. The spectators were drenched on their long journeys home. But, they agreed, it had been a night to remember.

Hours later a female serval, one of those small and graceful predators of the night, found an unexpectedly tasty morsel. It was Moloro's left foot.

"Ogwal, I am pleased with you," said Amin. "Now I have another task for you."

"Any task for you, Mr. Exalted President, is a pleasure."

"Of course," said Amin. "Our glorious victory over the invaders from Tanzania should be celebrated properly. We should have a great parade. See to it."

"Certainly, Mr. Exalted President," said Ogwal.

* * *

BARBRA EUGENIA KORCZYC: All the early years are blurred. They were washed away, deliberately washed away. Now I cannot tell what I remember of them and what I merely think I remember. The pieces I have been told by my brother Jan and by my mother, my real mother at the village of Rogonzo in Poland. The pieces I have learned from the International Red Cross woman and from my other mother, my mother in Germany. They have jumbled into each other, all those pieces, and they have become confused with what I sometimes think are real memories.

But, really, it makes very little difference for the facts are the facts and nothing can change them.

My father—my real father, that is—worked on a farm and he died in 1941 just a few months before I was born. Jan was only seven then and they were hard times in Rogozno.

In October, 1943, we were pulled out of our beds

very early in the morning by men in German uniforms. My mother was weeping and pleading, begging them not to take her children. But they did take us—first to a big hall in the middle of the village, where there were many other frightened children, and then on to the railway station.

Some of the women of the village tried to stop the train leaving. They linked their arms and formed a barrier across the rails in front of it. And the Germans hit them away with their rifles.

And 200,000 of us children were taken in that way from Poland. We were taken because we were considered intelligent and good-looking. We were to be brought up in Germany—indoctrinated into believing we were Germans—so that, in time, we could be sent to the human stud-farms which were being set up by the Third Reich. It was just part of Hitler's Lebensborn plan—a scheme to mass-produce the master race.

My family, like most others in that part of the country, could speak two languages—Polish and German. Now we children were ordered to speak only German. We were to forget all about our Polish past.

We were taken, at first, to a convent somewhere in Germany where we were looked after by nuns. They treated us with great kindness.

Then we were split into batches and I did not see Jan again until long after the war. Until 1948, it was. And by that time I had forgotten I had a brother.

For six months, or perhaps a little longer, I was in an orphanage with other little ones. People would come sometimes to choose children and take them away. And then it was my turn. A couple called Rademacher came to inspect me. The woman cuddled me and she laughed and nodded at her husband. And so they adopted me and took me back to their beautiful home by the Rhine at Coblenz. He was important in the Nazi party, this handsome new father of mine, and

*he believed what he had been told at the orphanage—
that my mother had died in childbirth and that my
father was a German officer who had been murdered
by Polish terrorists. This is what I believed also, for I
had been told it so often, and I hated the Polish people
for murdering the father I could not remember.*

*They were good to me, the Rademachers. They had
no children of their own and they loved me as a
daughter. And I loved them. He would be away often,
fighting in a distant war which I did not understand,
but he would always come back. And he would bring
me presents and take me on his knee and tell me such
wonderful stories . . .*

*Early in 1945 he was killed in action. And, after
that, the bond between me and my German mother
was even stronger. We clung to each other in our grief.*

*Germany was defeated and for a while Coblenz was
run by the Americans. There was a curfew, with Germans not being allowed in the streets after eight in the
evening, and there were great shortages of food. My
German mother often spoke about the women who sold
themselves to the Americans for butter or for bars of
chocolate. But they were not bad men, the American
soldiers. They were always generous to us children.*

*Then came the French and they were more harsh.
They threw people out of their homes, giving them only
ten minutes or so to pack what they could, so that they
could use them for themselves and their families. They
claimed priority on all public transport and sometimes
we would be ordered off to make space for them. They
built de-lousing stations on both banks of the Rhine and
all Germans who wanted to cross, by ferry or by bridge,
had to go through the humiliation of being "cleaned"
first.*

*We hated the French as we had never hated the
Americans. But the more they tormented us the more
proud we were of being Germans.*

My German mother explained to me that, although we had lost, we had lost honourably. Our soldiers had never behaved in such a barbarous manner. In the occupied territories they had always treated the civilians with compassion and humanity—despite the ridiculous stories being spread by the Allies.

"You must always be proud of being a German," she said.

In March, 1948, a strange woman came to our house. She was a representative, she said, of the International Red Cross and she started saying things that seemed like madness. She talked about a place called Rogozno and about some mad peasant woman in Poland who thought she was my mother.

My German mother smiled at first and explained quietly that there had been some mistake. Then she started getting angry and began swearing at the woman and telling her not to say such wicked things. The woman went away after about an hour and I was frightened and clung to my German mother. "Don't fret yourself, my baby," she said. "No-one's going to take you from me."

Three days later the woman came back and this time she had a boy with her. He was aged fourteen and she said he was my brother. This boy—Jan—started talking about Rogozno and about the old woman in Poland . . .

I did not believe anything they said. I knew about the Polish people. They were all dirty degenerates. They were vicious and evil. It was the Polish people who had killed my first father.

They looked sad, the woman and the boy, but finally they left. They came back twice more but after that they never returned to the house.

Letters addressed to me started to arrive from Poland. Many letters. My German mother tore them up. She said it was better for me not to read them. They would only upset me.

My German mother died in September, 1959. I was eighteen and, with no relatives left in Germany, I thought it might be interesting to see this strange old woman in Poland. All through the years, although she'd never had a reply, she had persisted in writing and sending pictures of herself. And I had a curiosity about her. That's all. Just a curiosity.

I was in Rogozno for at least two months before I started to recognise the terrible truth about myself, and the terrible wrong that had been done to my Polish mother.

Then I felt a hatred more overwhelming than I had ever known before. Against the Reich. Against Hitler and all he had represented. And I was thankful that my German mother had died without knowing the real truth. For I still loved my dead German mother.

I had to learn the Polish language. It is a difficult language to learn. Niedziela means Sunday. Poniedzialek means Monday. Wtorek means . . .

It is a very difficult language. But I worked hard and I learned it within three months. And then, with the guidance of my brother Jan, I was able to continue with my education at the Academy of Sciences in Plac Defilad, Warsaw.

My speciality is the maintenance of aircraft but, perhaps because of what has happened to me, I am also a keen student of world affairs. I am fearful of dictatorships and I am very conscious of the growing dangers . . .

In May, 1975, I was listening to a speech being made by Edward Gierek, our Head of State. We were celebrating the thirtieth anniversary of our victory over Fascism and he was applauding the progress of friendship between East and West.

"We hope this trend will continue successfully," he said. "This is necessary for peace in the world, for preventing a global nuclear conflagration."

He was being sincere. No question about it. But I could not help wondering if he had stopped to really think about the possible consequences of the help which we and other Eastern countries were giving to places like Uganda.

Some of my colleagues—who, like me, had been to Russia for special training—were already in Uganda as technical advisers. I knew that my turn would very likely come soon and I was uneasy.

I felt that Amin, in his way, represented as great a threat to world peace as Hitler ever had.

I mentioned these fears of mine—discreetly, of course—to an Englishman when I was with a trade delegation in London. He had lived near us in Coblenz after the war and he was a friend I could trust with my confidences.

The following day he telephoned me to say he would like me to meet an American. It might be good for business, he said.

The American was called Stanton.

* * *

"That's a bad habit of yours," said Theodor. "Biting your fingernails. It's very irritating."

"Not my fingernails." Lajeba was just slightly indignant. "Just bits of dead skin, that's all."

"It's still very irritating."

They were in the room at the Palace which had once been used by Moloro. Now it was Theodor's room. Theodor was stretched fully-dressed on the bed and Lajeba was comfortable in an armchair with his feet resting on a low stool.

"He was a thoroughly evil man—I know that—but I can't help feeling just a little guilty over him," said Theodor thoughtfully.

"Moloro?"

"Of course Moloro. It was a terrible way to go, wasn't it?" He got off the bed, feeling uncomfortably conscious that it had once been the sanctuary of the man who had died in that bed-cage in the sky. He, Theodor, had manipulated that man into the cage.

"Don't go wasting sentiment on Moloro," said Lajeba. "He had a great send-off, and it was far more humane than some he'd fixed for other people. And many of those people, don't forget, hadn't done any sort of wrong."

"Yes . . . I suppose . . ."

"No supposing about it, my friend. Did you know he was a great fan of Chairman Mao?"

"So?"

"Well, remember the infamous Mao dictum? In war there should be no scruples about benevolence, righteousness or morality. That's what Mao said and that's what Moloro believed. We're in a war here, Theodor, and we can't afford the luxury of a conscience—even if it were justified."

"They were good fireworks though, weren't they?" said Theodor inconsequentially.

"Very good fireworks indeed," agreed Lajeba.

Theodor got back on the bed. Lajeba, he could see, was right. It wasn't a question of killing one man . . . or five . . . or ten. It was a question of saving thousands and, very possibly, millions. Rather like swatting mosquitoes to stop them spreading some murderous malaria. That was what the Sanity International operation was all about and it was also giving him the satisfaction of proving to himself that he was not really a coward.

Anyway, this was now his bed. There was no longer such a person as Moloro.

"What's this parade going to be like?" he asked. "The one Ogwal's fixing."

"The victory celebrations? Oh, the usual, I imagine,"

said Lajeba. "A fly-past . . . a show of tanks . . . military bands . . . bags of pomp and swagger. And an excuse for people to wear their medals. You know—the usual. Still . . . some of the servants are grateful for it because of the boot-bonus."

"What on earth is the boot-bonus?"

"I thought you knew. It's something they can thank Ogwal for. Or, at least, they can thank his fatness. For every really flash parade like this, every really prestige one, all the top men get brand-new boots. Ogwal introduced the tradition to suit himself. He's so heavy on boots . . . sorry if that sounds like stating the obvious . . . but he *is* so heavy on boots that he keeps needing new ones. I'm told he got a bit of a complex about it, about himself needing new ones more often than anyone else and so he started this system of new boots for everyone. All the top men—they get them for every big parade."

"Whether they need them or not?"

"Absolutely."

"How very quaint."

"And you ought to see the scenes in the boot-room the night before any big parade," went on Lajeba. "The boys are there polishing and spitting on them and brushing and burnishing. It goes on for hours. And when they've finished those boots are like mirrors."

"And all this goes on the night before a parade?"

"Only before the big parades. When the boots have passed inspection—and that's usually in the early hours of the morning—they're left outside the doors for the body-servants to take in . . ."

"You still haven't told me about the boot-bonus. Not about why it pleases the servants so much."

"Only some of the servants," corrected Lajeba. "Personal body-servants, mostly. They keep getting the cast-off boots from their masters . . . and the old boots, as they're usually hardly worn, can fetch a good price in

Kampala market. I've often wondered how many peasants are tramping around in the President's old boots."

"Funny," said Theodor reflectively. "I'd never really thought of Ogwal as a charitable institution."

* * *

"This brother Jan you keep talking about—you think a lot of him, don't you?" Pierre Rey was inspecting a stuffed olive as if suspicious that it might be flawed. He decided it was perfect and flipped it into his mouth.

"He has done a great deal for me," said Barbra. "Anyway, it is right for one to like one's brother."

They were in a secluded corner of the Metropolitan bar. The hotel seemed quieter, gloomier, than usual. "Maybe," said Pierre. He suddenly appeared to be bored with the subject. "I still think we should go back to my bungalow," he said. "We can drink there and it's far cosier than this place.

Barbra sipped her gin-and-tonic thoughtfully. "Do you have any family?" she asked. "Any brothers or sisters?"

"Not to speak of," said Pierre. "Just a brother. A twin, would you believe."

"A twin! Why, that is wonderful. You never mentioned him before."

"We're not exactly close," said Pierre. "His name's Marcel, he's an archaeologist and he's a bore. He's got a pretty wife he doesn't deserve and he's the dreariest man you could imagine."

"Oh," said Barbra.

"Yes, that's brother Marcel," said Pierre. "He leads his life and I lead mine and that's the way I like it."

"Do you keep in touch?" asked Barbra.

"Not usually." Pierre chose another olive. "But it's strange you should ask." The olive, he decided, wasn't really up to standard and he put it back in the dish. "Only this morning I got a postcard from him. It seems he's in Cairo."

"He travels a great deal?"

"All over," said Pierre. "Last I heard of him he was in Turkey and before that it was God-knows-where. He travels on his wife's money, you know. He married a rich woman, that's what he did. And now he goes around the world spending her money."

"You really don't like him much, do you?"

"As I said, he's a bore. A long-suffering, sanctimonious bore. Still, I suppose he has his uses."

"Is it long since you've seen him?"

"Oh, ages. Ages and ages. But in fact I will be seeing him in London in November."

"What will you be doing in London?"

He looked annoyed. All these blasted questions. "Nothing important. Forget it," he said abruptly. "Now, about coming to my bungalow . . ."

She finished her drink. "You did promise that you'd show me over your aeroplane."

"It's not my aeroplane," he replied. "It's the President's."

"You still promised."

"God, but you're persistent! I suppose you want to go right now?"

She stood up. "Why not?" she said.

*   *   *

Theodor was fast asleep. He was dreaming of Munich and of his dead wife Sybille. Sometimes in his dreams Sybille was drinking or dying. But she was not drinking in this dream. She was young and radiant in a summer dress and they were strolling hand-in-hand through a beautifully-tended park. They were as they had been early in their marriage . . . secure in their happiness and their love . . .

Suddenly he was aware of someone roughly shaking his shoulder. He tried to clutch at the dream, tried to snuggle back into it, but the shaking went on.

The light had been turned on and he blinked owlishly in its glare. And then he saw the panic in Lajeba's eyes.

"Quickly!" said Lajeba. "It's an attempt on Amin's life. We can't waste a second!"

Theodor flung back his covers and, still wearing only his pyjama trousers, ran after Lajeba into the corridor.

CHAPTER 5

Dr. Hugo Engelman, chief medical advisor for the Sanity International operation, was as tall and skinny as a plucked crane. A permanently angry-looking crane. Most of the people in Chicago, he was convinced, were hypochondriacs or fools or both. He had little patience with them and he also had an ulcer.

He was, however, an exceptionally talented doctor. That's why Stanton had picked him.

Stanton drummed his fingers on the huge glass-topped desk. He seemed uncharacteristically anxious. "We are positive, aren't we, Hugo? I mean one hundred per cent, rock-solid positive. This is the one segment of the whole caboodle that keeps niggling at me. If we're wrong on this one point—"

"I'm not in the habit of screwing up medical facts," said Engelman tersely. "Go get a second opinion if you don't trust me."

"Now, now . . . please . . . Hugo. That's not how it is and you know it. It's just that Pierre Rey and his kidneys—they're the key to the whole thing."

"I had a patient in this morning," said Engelman. "He came in and told me—told *me,* if you please— what he'd diagnosed about himself. And then he told me how I should be treating him. He'd read all about it in some magazine. I nearly told him to screw off and treat himself if he was so goddamned smart."

"Hugo . . . I wasn't trying to imply . . ."

"Would have done, as well," went on Engelman.

"Would have told him to screw off out of it. But he'd got his diagnosis so wrong you'd never believe . . ."

"All I wanted you to say, Hugo, is that we really are positive."

Engelman glared at him for a moment and then suddenly smiled indulgently. He lounged back in the low chair facing the desk and crossed his long and elegantly-trousered legs. "I told you that already," he said. "I told you three times, for Chrissakes. Without Marcel there's no transplant and without the transplant Pierre dies. There! It's that simple."

"Sure, Hugo, thanks. I guess I just wanted reassuring."

Engelman sighed and uncrossed his legs. "I'll give you it all again," he said. "I'll give you it in detail. Then you'll never need reassuring again. Okay?"

And, before Stanton could reply, he started ticking the facts off on his fingers in his sternest lecture-room style.

"One—Pierre Rey can still function normally at the moment and he is managing to keep his condition a secret from those around him. But it wouldn't be long before his condition started to deteriorate. And then it would start to deteriorate so fast that he'd soon have to be plugged into a kidney machine two or three times a week. Ergo, end of career."

Up went a second bony finger. "Two—Marcel Rey has agreed to donate a kidney and the transplant's due to take place in London in November. This Pierre's a very lucky boy because there's a chronic shortage of kidney donors."

He paused as if challenging Stanton to dispute the fact, but Stanton stayed silent.

"There were about twenty thousand kidney transplants across the world last year and there'd have been forty or fifty thousand if the kidneys had been available," went on Engelman.

Up with the third finger. "Three—he's doubly lucky, this Pierre, because he's being given it by his brother. The usual success rate for these transplants is only seventy per cent or less when the donor is a non-relative. It goes up to ninety per cent when the kidney comes from someone in the family.

"So okay—Pierre's got it all going for him. But take away Marcel and see what happens. He's in the most goddamned awful mess, that's what happens. He's far worse off than almost any other man would be.

"If it was you or me Stanton we might . . . and I wouldn't pitch it any higher than that . . . we might get a kidney from some other source. With our Pierre there's no chance of that because of his blood group . . ."

"Yes, that I have got clear," said Stanton. "And . . ."

Engelman waved imperiously for silence and stood up. "I said I'd give you it in detail, all the detail," he said. "So, whether you've got it clear or not, you just listen. I don't want any more of that 'are we positive' stuff. It gets me mad, that sort of talk."

"Well, I did apologise," said Stanton.

"Screw your apologies. Just listen," said Engelman. "Pierre and Marcel, as I told you before, have both got AB blood and that's got no agglutins in the plasma.

"Only two per cent of the population have that blood. Then Pierre and Marcel both have the complication of the Rhesus negative factor—something found in only sixteen per cent of people.

"So you start permutating the AB and the Rhesus—multiplying up the two per cent with the sixteen per cent—and you see the score.

"You've got that boy Pierre locked up like a monkey in a barrel. Without his brother Marcel he's got no chance. He's as good as dead and, what's more, he knows it."

"Thank you," said Stanton. "That's what I wanted to hear. Now it's all in perspective."

"I should hope so too," said Engelman. "Now, are you going to offer me a drink or do I have to go out and buy my own?"

*　　*　　*

JAMES WEAVER: My dad, looking back on it now, was a kink. In fact, because of him and his oddities, we were a screwball sort of household. You don't see those things until you're much older and can get them into some sort of perspective. When you're a kid you get trapped in it all and take it as normal.

We lived in Paddington, one of the older parts of Sydney, in a sombre and respectable sort of house with cast-iron ornamental railings at the front to keep out the world. And my folks, I suppose, were just about the most un-Australian couple in the whole of Australia.

He worked in a bank, my dad, and he was a walking mix of inhibitions. Just about the most crabby, tight-lipped character you could ever hope to meet. I don't think I ever heard him laugh, not really laugh, and it was the law in our house that he was always right. No matter what he did, said or thought—he was always right.

My mother was a house-mouse. Always nervous and timid. Always scuttling around trying to anticipate his wishes. When he was at home she would almost tip-toe around so as not to disturb him. I was scared of him when I was small but I swear she was even more scared. If he'd told her it was immoral for her to be seen breathing in public, she'd have done her best to break the habit.

He was very strong on morals, my dad. He didn't approve of gambling or smoking or boozing. He didn't approve of the noisy nut-brown extroverts who enjoyed life all around us and he warned me against growing up like them. "Babylon," he used to say. "Remember what happened to Babylon." I wasn't too clear, at that

119

time, what Babylon was and he never explained, but it sounded very important and rather nasty.

On Sunday afternoons he often used to talk, in capital letters, about the Hell Fires of Judgement Day and about the Wrath of Almighty God. You'd never believe the nightmares I had as a kid because of the Wrath of Almighty God.

I'll tell you something else, as well, about him. I don't reckon there could be any other man as self-conscious about his bodily functions. About opening his bowels and that. You know what? He was so self-conscious that he'd never go to the lavatory—not if he could avoid it—until the rest of the house was asleep. I know it sounds crazy but that's how it was. If he had to go, I mean, if he was busting, he'd go sneaking off and pretend he was going somewhere else.

In fact, this business of pretending he was going somewhere else . . . he was better at it than I realised.

It wasn't until I was grown-up and married myself that I learned the truth about his Saturday afternoons. I'd always believed what he'd said—about him having to put in extra hours at the bank. It was a jolt when I found out about King's Cross.

King's Cross, you must understand, is the most explosively jam-packed bit of Sydney. All bustle and clamour. All espresso bars and over-full pubs. Neon lights and juke-boxes. Hunched-up little shops and foreign restaurants—all huddled around the golden fountain at the center. That is the heart of King's Cross. And, just away from it all, are the narrow streets where rooms are rented by the hour and questions are not asked.

The whores there work on a cut-price, quick-turn-over basis.

Maybe that's why my dad was so pre-occupied by the Hell Fires of Judgement Day on Sunday afternoons.

May, 1950. He has never before talked to me about sex. Sex, like lavatories, is a taboo subject. Now, early

*in the evening, he has forced himself to come to my
room to do what he clearly sees as his duty. A man-to-
man talk. A facts-of-life talk.*

*"Jim," he says. "You are eleven years of age and
you are growing up. There are things that, as your
father, I've got to talk to you about."*

*I lie there in my bed, half guessing at what is coming
and dreading it perhaps even more than he does. I say
nothing and there is a long embarrassed silence. "Yes,
Dad?" I say eventually.*

*"You are growing up into a young man and there
are things you ought to know—about how to behave
and how not to behave." He can't bring himself to look
at me as he talks. "I'm sure you're a good boy but
there's something that, if I didn't tell you about, I
wouldn't be doing my duty."*

*I wait and, for a while, it seems as if he has decided
to say no more. Then he goes to the foot of the bed,
crosses his arms, and says in a sudden and quick voice:
"Don't play with yourself Jim. Never play with yourself. It's bad for you."*

*Now I feel shocked and hot and guilty. "But I don't,
Dad." My protest sounds small and unconvincing.
"Honest—I don't."*

*He moves with jerky self-consciousness towards the
door, obviously anxious to escape downstairs. "No, I'm
sure you don't," he says. "You've been well brought-up
in this house and you're a good boy. And boys who
play with themselves are doing wicked things."*

*I wait for him to talk about the Wrath of Almighty
God like he does on Sundays. But he doesn't mention
Almighty God.*

*"Well, that's it then," he says. "You know now, so I
won't need to mention it again." And, without another
word, he leaves the room.*

*I've heard at school, of course, about what it can
do to you. Ginger Newton, the oldest boy in the class
and the first to grow pubic hair, has explained it all*

*to us. It can make you go blind and insane and it can
give you a bad back. It makes us feel we are living
dangerously, the way Ginger Newton puts it.*

*But now I begin to wonder if there might not con-
ceivably be even greater dangers. Perhaps there is a
special corner of hell reserved for eleven-year-old boys
who masturbate . . .*

*August, 1956. There's this joke in Sydney about the
man taking a census. He asks the housewife how many
children she's got and she says: "Seven. One in Melbourne and six still living." That joke just about sums
up what Sydneysiders think about Melbourne. They
tend to write it off as a gigantic concrete morgue, popu-
lated exclusively by stiff shirts and the pompous living
dead. And this traditional dislike is a two-way business.
Melbournians, in general, are disparaging about the
people of Sydney. They see them as flash, arrogant and
vulgar. There's only four hundred miles or so between
the cities but moving from one to the other is like
moving to another world. And that's just what we're
doing. Dad's got a new job with a bank in Melbourne.
It's promotion, he says.*

*So we're away from the sombrely-respectable house
in Paddington and getting ourselves settled into an even
more sombrely-respectable house—built by some rich
and no-nonsense Victorian—near the Yarra River in
Melbourne. There's nothing beautiful about this river,
not as I see it. It's so murky and brown that folks say
it got confused, many years ago, and started running
upside down.*

*Anyway, here we are. Melbourne. And nothing much
changes. Dad still goes off on Saturdays and he still
talks about Hell Fires on Sundays. And soon I'm leaving school and starting my apprenticeship as a surveyor.
It's in the surveyor's office that I first meet Rita. She's
Mr. Foggatty's typist so we work together a lot but I
don't get round to saying much to her for a while. It's
not that I don't want to. I mean, she's really pretty, but
I've never found it too easy to talk to girls . . .*

February, 1959. She looks scared when she tells me and I suppose, when the news sinks in, I look just as scared. Pregnant! How the hell can I tell my dad I've got a girl pregnant? Stupid, isn't it. It's not her I'm thinking about. Not Rita. Not even myself. I'm just thinking about my dad and how he'll take the news. Jesus, he'll go raving bloody mad.

" 'Course I'm sure," she says crossly. "You think I'd say so if I wasn't sure?"

And I apologise because I know it was a stupid question.

"What are we going to do about it?" she asks.

"What the fuck can we do about it?"

"There's no need to swear. You've never sworn before—not like that."

"I've never had such bloody cause before."

And, later, we are smoking cigarettes and trying to think about it dispassionately. An innocence child. That's what it is—an innocence child. If only my dad had talked to me about contraception instead of masturbation . . .

In a way, perhaps we've been lucky that this hasn't happened earlier. That first time, with us hidden in the long grass beyond the gidgee shrubs . . . it had been the first time for both of us. It just happened, that first evening, and then it went on happening. And in our explorations we'd never even considered what the result could be.

I stub my cigarette. "Sod my father!" I say. "Will you marry me?"

"Do you really want me to?"

"Of course I bloody want you to."

And I mean it as well. It's not just because of the baby. I love this girl.

October, 1965. "Do you know," says my daughter Karen, "that one rabbit can eat more grass than seven sheep." She nods her head emphatically, as if worried that I might challenge the fact. "That's absolutely true," she says. "We were told that at school."

She is six now and it is obvious that, one day, she will be as beautiful a woman as her mother. And I can't help thinking, as I've thought so often before, that the accident behind the gidgee shrubs was probably the luckiest thing that ever happened to me. If it hadn't been for that I might never have married Rita.

Rita is down there below us, at the foot of the ridge, packing the picnic stuff into the station-waggon. The Dandenong mountains. This is our favourite Saturday place, a place for relaxing and switching off from the week. There is no sound here now, except for the plain-tive melody of a distant bird. "That's a currawong," *says Karen.* "It's a sort of crow."

"And I suppose that's something else you've learned in school." *I grin at her.* "Come on, baby. Time for home."

I scoop her up and she shrieks with excitement as I run to the station-waggon with her in my arms. Jesus, but life is good.

We have this sprawling sort of bungalow place with a fair bit of land and ramshackle out-buildings, just south-east of Melbourne, and it takes us a little under an hour to get back there. A policeman is waiting on the drive-way and his face is serious. "Mr. James Weaver?"

"Sure . . . Jim Weaver . . . that's me."

"I'm afraid I've got bad news for you, Mr. Weaver." *He glances meaningfully at Karen and Rita, taking the hint, hustles her indoors.*

"Your father is dead," *says the policeman.* "Heart attack. He died two hours ago."

"Christ, no! How's my mum . . .?"

"Your mother doesn't know yet." *There's a strange look in his eyes.* "We felt that, in the circumstances, it might be better to tell you first . . ."

"What circumstances? What the hell are you talking about?"

"Doctor says it was natural causes, so maybe your

*mother doesn't need to know all the facts," says the
policeman. "That's why we reckoned it best to tell you
first—so that you can decide."*

"Will you please tell me what you are trying to say!"
I'm doing my best not to sound agitated and my voice
sounds unnaturally hoarse. "Is there something unusual
about the way my father died?"

"He was in bed with a woman."

*"But that's not possible. Not my father. Listen . . .
you sure you haven't got the wrong man? It couldn't be
my father. And, anyway, it's Saturday afternoon. He's
always at the bank on Saturday afternoons. He works
extra time at the bank . . ."*

The policeman shakes his head and then braces his
shoulders to make himself seem taller. "I'll put it on
the line, Mr. Weaver," he says. "Your father hasn't
been working extra time at the bank. Not on Saturdays.
I'm sorry but . . . well . . . it's best for you to know.
Your father died in a brothel. He was in bed at the time
with a woman called Fay."

"Oh, now come on . . ."

Rita comes out looking anxious and I wave her back
into the bungalow. "You stay with Karen," I says. "I'll
be in in a moment."

*"She's very shaken up, this Fay," says the policeman.
"I think—believe it or not—she was really quite fond
of him."*

This is getting more and more incredible. It's my
father *we're* talking about. My crabby tight-lipped
father with his hell-fire talk and his inhibitions.

*"Then she knew him? I mean, he'd been there be-
fore?"*

He nods sadly. "Just about every Saturday for the
last three years. Fay was his usual but if she wasn't
around he'd have one of the others. There are six of
them in the house."

"Christ—no!" I can imagine my mum listening to all
this and I am glad the policeman has come to me first.

"*This Fay—what's she like?*" It's such a stupid and irrelevant question but I can't think what else to say. "*She pretty?*"

He shrugs noncommittally. "*What about your mother?*" he says. "*What do you want to tell her?*"

"*She needn't know, need she? I mean, not where and how?*"

"*That's up to you,*" he says. "*That's why we're telling you first.*"

"*Then I'll tell her it was at the bank. It's best for her to think that.*"

I have to identify the body. He is naked and grey in the mortuary and somehow he looks smaller than he did in life. And I have no pity for him. Only contempt.

"*No, Jim, don't try to hide the truth from me,*" says my mum later. "*He wasn't at the bank. He never went to the bank on Saturdays.*"

"*But of course he did. You remember . . . even when I was a kid and we lived in Sydney . . .*"

"*Yes, it was the same then,*" says my mum. "*He never went to the bank on Saturdays then either. There was a time when I believed he really was going to the bank and I used to worry about him working too hard. I even tried to stop him once because I thought he was working too hard. Then my brother Sammy saw him— going into that house at King's Cross.*"

"*Jesus, mum! You knew! All these bloody years you knew—and you never said a word.*"

"*He was a good man,*" says my mum. "*It was just that he had these needs. I loved him . . . and I was frightened he'd be too ashamed to come back if he knew I knew.*

"*Tell me about today . . . I'm right, aren't I? He was with a girl? When he died, I mean. He was with a girl?*"

She seems so calm . . . so strangely dignified . . . and her tranquillity angers me. "*So all along you've known just what sort of a filthy, stinking, hypocritical old sod he was and—*"

"Now, Jim," says my mum softly. *"I don't want you talking like that. He was always a good father to you."*

I met this feller once who said he was just waiting for his boss to die . . . so that he could go along and piss on his grave. I thought then that was a terrible thing to say. But now I can understand it. My father— what a bastard . . .

March, 1973. The husband, they say, is always the last to know. And that's how it is with me. My friends, it seems, have been aware of it for weeks. Maybe for months. But me—no. I don't even suspect a bloody thing. If you'd asked me a week ago—or even yesterday, come to that—I'd have told you I'd got a great marriage. One of the best. And, by Christ, I'd have meant it.

I didn't know about this Porter feller then. About him and Rita.

My work takes me away a fair bit and right now I'm up for a month in Broken Hill. It's stuck out in the desert, Broken Hill, and it's just about the craziest mining town in the world. It's a sewn-up sort of town, about 400 miles from Melbourne and a good 200 miles from the next bit of civilisation, where the locals make their own laws—and where strangers just aren't welcome. No-one is allowed to work in the Broken Hill mines unless he has been born and bred in Broken Hill. It's that tight a community. And men like me, staying for a special contract job, are constantly reminded that we are outsiders. "Ring-tails"—that's the local word for us foreigners.

There are two of us ring-tails there together from Melbourne—me and another surveyor called Sharp. He's not my sort of feller, this Sharp but—what with the way things are in Broken Hill—we're more or less pushed into spending our spare time together. And it's Sharp who tells me about Porter.

He says he hopes I won't get the wrong idea, that I won't think he's trying to make trouble. It's just that he *feels it's something I should know. And I feel like smashing in his face.*

But then, when I'm on my own, I get to thinking. And I can see, although it pulls my guts apart to admit it, that it could add up.

That time in January when I got back from Mildura . . . Rita was acting a bit strange then. Sort of nervy and on the defensive. And then there was that funny business about her having to visit her sick cousin in Orbost. At the time I couldn't figure out why she needed to spend a week there. It wasn't as if she had ever been close to her cousin.

On impulse, I put through a call to Rita's cousin in Orbost. It bemuses her, of course. She can't understand why I should be calling for a social chit-chat and she probably thinks I'm boozed up. But I don't give a damn what she thinks and I slip in the questions carefully so she doesn't even notice them. And then I know that Sharp was telling the truth. Rita never went to Orbost.

I try to call home and there's no reply. Very odd. I mean, she's just got to be there. Karen should be having her tea by now and . . .

I call my mum. Karen, it seems, is staying there for a couple of nights. "No, nothing to be alarmed about," says my mum. "Rita's feeling a bit tired, that's all. And she feels that a few days on her own will do her the world of good . . ."

A few days on her own! So it really is true! The scheming, steaming cow! She's got me out of the way and Karen out of the way. And now she's with this Porter. What did she do last night? Spend it with him in my bed? And what about tonight? The same? I can almost see them coupling on my mattress. My Rita and this unknown Porter. I can almost feel his semen spurting into her. And I let out a howl of despair and murderous rage.

It is long after midnight before I get back to the

bungalow. My headlights dazzle off the windows as I turn into the drive-way and I suppose that is what warns him. Gravel spurts noisily as I slam on the brakes and, just as I am getting out of the station-waggon, I see him running from the side door. It's too dark to make out any features. There's just this shadowy figure scuttling from the bungalow to the old stable—and I charge after him.

He hears me coming after him. And, as I step through the open door into the blackness, he smashes his fist into my face. Blood is oozing down my face as I grapple with him and then his knee jolts into my groin. I almost retch over his shoulder in my agony but I still cling on. His left arm is now around me, pinning me to him, and his right thumb-nail is gouging at my left eye.

My hands reach his throat and, in fear and desperation, I squeeze. There's a sudden violent pain in my left eye and all I want to do now is escape. I want to tear myself away from him but he's too strong and he won't let me go. So I grip even tighter on his neck. And suddenly it happens. He goes limp and sags against me, before sliding awkwardly to the ground. I can't take it in at first. But it's true. I've killed him.

My own pain is instantly forgotten. I run to the bungalow, shouting for Rita. But she's not there. Nobody's there. The place is in a hell of a state. Drawers ransacked. Stuff strewn everywhere. Just like it's been hit by a whirlwind. And there, neat in the centre of my pillow, is an envelope.

I can't see out of my left eye any more. There's no pain, just a sort of blank numbness, but it seems to be completely blind. I rip open the letter. It's from Rita and it's dated two days ago.

I have to screw up my right eye to focus on the words: ". . . sorry to have to do this to you, darling, but Frank and I are so hopelessly in love . . . he's got a new job in Brisbane so I'll call you from there in about a *week . . . we must do what is best for Karen . . . please try to understand . . ."*

And by now the man in the stable—just a thief who'd picked the wrong empty house—is starting to get colder.

I don't know what to do. I'm bloody and half-blind. I've lost my wife and I've killed a strange man. And I sit down in the devastation of my home and I cry like a kid. I just don't know what to do.

Coffee and a cigarette. They help pull me together. And now I'm starting to think more rationally. I can't blame myself for killing the man. That was an accident and, anyway, it was his fucking fault for breaking into my home. I have to get rid of the body.

I'm sweating like a pig as I hump him into the back of the station-waggon. Then I cover him, and my spade, with an old rug before setting off for the Dandenongs.

It's strange, in a way, isn't it—that I should bury him so near to what had been our favourite Saturday place.

It's nearly 5 a.m. when I get back to the bungalow. I call the police and tell them how I got back unexpectedly from Broken Hill and surprised an intruder who attacked me and then escaped . . .

And they tell me not to worry because they're sure they'll find him. And I hope to Christ they don't.

"Sorry," says the doctor later. "But it's going to be a glass eye. There's nothing else we can do." And somehow it doesn't seem too bad. There are worse things in the world than a glass eye.

Karen stays with my mum for a while. Then Rita says she's still really serious about this Porter feller. They're going to get married just as soon as our divorce comes through. And, with it being as definite as that, there seems no point in me being difficult. So I give my permission and Karen goes off to live with them in Brisbane. I miss her, of course, but it seems best for the kid.

And now I want to get away from it all. I want to get the hell out of Australia and start afresh.

I sell the bungalow and decide to try my luck in America. There's an old mate of mine doing nicely for himself over there—in Chicago, Illinois. He helps me get on my feet there and introduces me around.

One of the people he introduces me to is a man called Stanton.

*   *   *

High over the peak of the next mountain, just below the straggling wisps of white cloud, the lonely bird seemed motionless, like a midget black moth pinned to a painted sky. Suddenly it was swooping and swerving, presumably chasing its frightened breakfast. There was speed and lethal beauty in its hungry pursuit. Then it soared back to the heights and, once again, it was sitting, wings outstretched, on the broad shoulders of a thermal current.

Yvette, just outside the entrance of the first cave, was watching with drowsy half-interest. She had no idea what sort of bird it might be. Marcel, she thought sourly, would certainly know. All the tedious and irrelevant details about it would be catalogued somewhere in the back of his head. He'd probably be able to tell its ancestry . . . its age . . . its sex . . . and whether or not it had pimples on its knee-caps. Or did birds have knee-caps? She wasn't sure. In fact, she just didn't know. It was a piece of information she'd managed to live without, and anyway—like Marcel himself who was still snoring back in the inner cave—it was supremely unimportant.

Far below her, where the river wriggled through the green valley, she could see pastel clusters of pink oleander. Between her and the point where the rocks began diving so precipitously was the Moroccan sentry. He was some relative, as far as she could understand, of the man they called Tommy.

This particular sentry, she had decided, was quite

exceptionally surly. He would just sit there in hours of sullen silence, watching with resentful eyes as if he was blaming her for this dreary waste of his time. He never seemed to speak, not even to Tommy, and she wondered if perhaps he might be dumb as well as stupid. His manner made her feel strangely uncomfortable, as if there was some smouldering menace in it, and she tried to concentrate again on the distant peak. The bird was again slicing gracefully downwards through the sky . . .

Carter, obviously not long awake, came out of the cave with a mug of coffee.

"Morning, Dickie darling."

He grunted, shook his head as if to clear it, and sat close to her.

"You look miserable this morning."

"Not miserable," he said gruffly. "Just waking up." He fumbled in his pockets for cigarettes and matches. "I hate bloody mornings," he said.

"Particularly after an energetic night?"

He grinned ruefully. "Yes—particularly then."

He lit two cigarettes and gave her one. "You think he suspects?" he asked.

She pulled a face. "Why should he? He never has in the past."

"You make a habit of it, then?"

"I enjoy life, if that's what you mean. And you?"

He finished his coffee. "I get by," he said. "I enjoy the simple things."

"And these simples—do you tell *them* all the same silly story?" There was now a sharp edge to her voice. "Do you always lay claim to that ridiculous name? Or is that reserved for ones like me?"

"I'd hardly describe you as a simple thing," he hedged.

She moved nearer. "And that's ducking the question, isn't it?"

"What exactly was the question?"

"About your name, Dickie. I mean, it's quite funny, isn't it, in a pathetic sort of way. Richard Richards. It's so obvious, darling. Like Peter Peters or Smith Smiths. You really could have done better than that."

"Drop it, Yvette."

"Of course, Dickie darling." Her tone had become soothing and conciliatory. "If it pleases you to be Richard Richards, you go right on being Richard Richards. I wouldn't want to stop your pleasure in any way at all . . ."

"Just forget it, will you."

". . . and I shall go on thinking of you as Dickie darling. My own Dickie darling. Only, for more formal occasions, perhaps it should be Dickie Carter."

He jumped, startled, to his feet and leaned over her, his fists clenched in anger. "Where did you hear that name?"

"The name 'Carter'?"

"You know bloody well what I mean."

"Sit down, Dickie. You're so conspicuous up there." She waited. "There, that's better." She twined her fingers through his and began teasing them. "There's no need to be angry with your Yvette," she said coquettishly. "Why do you have to get in such a tizzy? You know my name—it's Yvette Rey. And you don't mind me knowing your body, every bit of your body, so why be so shy about your name?"

He detached his hand. "I'm serious, Yvette. Was it one of the others? Did you hear them mention it?"

"I wouldn't have been so curious, really I wouldn't, if it hadn't *seemed* such a silly name."

"I must know, Yvette. It's important."

She recaptured his hand. "Last night, my darling . . . afterwards . . . you were tired." She sighed with the pleasure of recollection. "It would have been remarkable if you hadn't been tired . . ."

"Go on," said Carter.

"Your trousers—they were right by us, right by our

side. It's a funny place, you know, to keep a driving licence—in the back pocket of your trousers."

"You bitch! You stupid bitch!"

"It could fall out of there or anything," she said calmly. "It is not a sensible place to keep it."

He felt in his buttoned-down back pocket. The licence was there. "So you put it back."

"Of course I put it back. I told you. I was curious, that's all—just curious."

"Don't mention this to anyone, not to anyone—understand?" He was now speaking quietly and urgently. "I don't want to scare you, Yvette, but let me spell out the facts for you. You and your husband will be in danger, really bad danger, if the others find out. Particularly the Australian. He's a bastard, that one and he's killed before."

"What are you two up to?"

Weaver, they were suddenly aware, was in the mouth of the cave just a little behind them.

"Talking," said Carter, without turning his head. "Just talking."

Weaver strolled over towards them. "You!" he said to Yvette. "Get back in there with your husband."

She turned to Carter for support but he was studiously looking away, aiming all his attention at the opposite mountain.

"Jump!" shouted Weaver. "Come on, shift your arse!"

She got up and, pouting, sauntered past him into the caves.

Weaver stood immediately behind Carter, looking down at the top of his head. "I warned you," he said. "She's married and I warned you to lay off her."

"I remember," said Carter. "I also remember telling you to piss off."

"One of these days . . ." Weaver began.

Carter got to his feet and turned to face him. "Yes? What?"

"One of these days you'll regret saying that," said Weaver. He looked, for a moment, as if he was going to add something but he changed his mind and walked back towards the caves. He could hear Carter taunting him. "Yes sir," Carter was saying. "Yes sir, Mr. Preacher Man . . ."

The Moroccan sentry, the cousin of Cherif, was watching them sullenly. He gave no indication of having heard a word.

* * *

They ran silently through the empty corridors until they reached the doorway to Amin's room. "There!" whispered Lajeba. He pointed at the gleaming new boots. "They've been doctored," he added. "And they're ready to kill."

"A bomb?"

"No . . . something much more traditional."

Theodor was still trying to catch his breath. "Tell me," he said.

"I was patrolling around, on and off, just like you told me to," said Lajeba. "On two occasions I noticed these boots. The second time it seemed that the right one had been moved. Only a fraction, but it had been moved."

"So?"

"So I examined it." He picked up the right boot. "It had been tampered with." He produced a knife and used its point to indicate a tiny, almost indiscernible mound in the leather on the inside of the heel. "Watch this."

With the knife he neatly lifted a corner of the inside leather skin and peeled it back. Theodor could still see nothing of significance. Lajeba tapped the knife gently at the centre of the exposed surface and there was just the faintest chink of metal against metal. "That's not a nail coming through," he said. "That's a barb. And don't touch it, because it's lethal."

"Poisoned?"

"An old Ugandan folk-trick," said Lajeba. "Not very original but very effective."

He stroked the solid heel of the boot. "There'll be a capsule fitted in here—that's the usual," he said. "A capsule of instant death. When the boot is being worn, that barb will slowly work its way through the leather strip. Then it will puncture the skin."

Theodor nodded gravely. "And the process, of course, would be much faster if the boot was being worn on a hard surface."

"Such as a military parade ground," agreed Lajeba.

"You've done well," said Theodor. "But now we've got to get the man responsible. He obviously has access to this part of the Palace and he can't be allowed to try again."

He raised his left wrist, forgetting for a moment that his watch was still in his room with his clothes. "What's the time?"

"Half past two," said Lajeba. "We've got about three hours before the Palace starts waking up."

"Who should be up and about at this time?"

"Well, the guards, of course, but—as you know— they're posted around the domestic area. They're normally not allowed inside it. Maybe a couple of the boot-boys are still up, doing the last few pairs. I doubt if anyone else is."

"Give me the knife," said Theodor. He picked up the left boot, the untampered one, and gashed its polished surface with the tip of the knife. "You take this boot and give me that right one," he said. "I'm going to my room to get dressed and I want you to bring me the chief boot-boy or whatever he's called. I don't care if he's in bed. I don't care what he's doing. Show him that mark on the President's boot and tell him I'm screaming mad about it. Tell him I'm holding him personally responsible. Put the fear of God into him and then bring him to me."

The head boot-boy, an elderly and tremulous man called Banwe, *was* terrified. He seemed to be anticipating almost instant decapitation and, as he trembled abjectly before Theodor, he could not stop stuttering. "B-but, p-please, honoured sir. I check every boot—before it leaves. Every b-boot—I check it myself."

"And the President's boots?"

"Especially, honoured sir. M-most especially the b-boots of the P-President. Those are cleaned by me. B-by me personally."

It seemed that he was ready to burst into tears. "Then the blame is all yours," said Theodor coldly. "This outrage, this insult to the dignity of the President—it is because of your carelessness. You hear me? The President of Uganda might even have been seen in public wearing damaged boots—all because of your laziness!"

"N-no, please, honoured sir. I swear the boot was undamaged when I p-polished it."

Banwe was now cringing in pitiful terror and Theodor was still trying to assess him. Could this creature possibly be part of an assassination attempt? Would any conspirators dare to put their trust in such a pathetic creature? The answers, he knew instinctively, had to be "no." But it was necessary for Banwe to be racked a little longer.

"Tell me about the boots," ordered Theodor. "How are they delivered, and from where? Are they identical in design? And, if they are, who decides which pair goes to the President?"

The answers satisfied him that the boots for Amin had been picked at random, from others of the same size, by Banwe. The chances of their having been "specially-treated" in the boot-room—or before delivery to the Palace—were too remote. It would have been far too easy for a mistake to have been made—for them to be delivered to the door of the wrong man.

He had still not mentioned the barb and the capsule of poison.

"Who actually put them outside the President's door?"

Banwe howled with despair.

"Come on, man! Who?"

"P-please, honoured sir. I also did that myself."

Theodor began to adopt a more conciliatory manner. "Then I suspect that you, Banwe, are the victim of a malicious and wicked plot," he said. "Someone is trying to steal your good reputation, to get you into the most serious of trouble."

Another despairing howl. Theodor waited briefly until the man was calmer.

"I believe you, Banwe," he said evenly. "I believe you are a man who tells the truth and so there can be only one explanation. Somebody else damaged the boots—or perhaps even changed them—after you left them so beautifully outside the door of the President."

Hope was starting to seep into Banwe's anxious eyes. Maybe, after all, this strange white man was not going to have him punished . . .

Theodor's next words crushed his hopes. "But the boots are still your responsibility and, for a crime such as this, there has to be retribution," said Theodor. "So you will find the guilty man. Some person was outside the President's door between the time you put the boots there and the time I saw them. Some person with no right to be there. Bring me that person."

"B-but honoured sir—"

Theodor, feeling uncomfortable in the severe role he was forcing himself to play, would not let him speak. "Wake up all your boys. Wake up all the servants if necessary. Question them all and go on questioning until you find the man. Somebody must have seen someone. They *must* have. And, if they didn't, then the blame comes back to you, Banwe. Have you ever seen a man with his ears cut off?"

"N-no . . . please . . ."

"Or his nose cut off? It is not pleasant, Banwe. You have exactly one hour to save yourself. Now go!"

And, after Banwe had scuttled from the room, Theodor turned gloomily to Lajeba. "Poor little man," he said. "I hated doing that. You know, I'm beginning to realise something. This business of protecting Amin from assassins is harder than organising his assassination and, in some ways, it is far more unpleasant."

"Not still thinking about Moloro?"

"No, not just Moloro. About the whole thing. It gets dirtier and dirtier."

"He really believed you, that one, about chopping off his nose and ears."

"Of course he believed me, and that's what makes it so awful. No man has the right to put that sort of fear into another."

"But isn't that one of the reasons we're here?" said Lajeba. "I saw that look of fear once—fear and abject hopelessness—in the eyes of my friend Amit. That's why I'm here. I'm here because of Amit and the people like him—and the people who could become like him in the future."

"You're right," said Theodor. "Come on, we're wasting time. Let's help Banwe chase up his boys . . ."

It was nearly four o'clock when Banwe returned to Theodor's room. His attitude was now very different. He was confident, jubilant almost, and he was no longer stuttering.

Two of his boot-boys were with him as an escort, helping him prod forward a young and straw-thin man who was completely naked.

"We wasted no time, honoured sir. We brought this man straight from his bed. His name is Mafale."

Here in Banwe, Theodor thought sadly, was a prime example of the cruelty within men. This head boot-boy, so petrified himself only a short time before, was now happy to be the tormentor. He had obviously enjoyed dragging this naked man from his bed. He was now revelling in his power over another frightened human being.

"There was no time for him to dress?" asked Theodor.

"We wasted no time, honoured sir," repeated Banwe importantly.

Theodor flung the coverlet from his bed at Mafale who gratefully wrapped it around himself.

"Tell me about him."

"He was in the corridor, honoured sir. This boy here saw him in the corridor. He had no right to be there, honoured sir, and he was carrying a pair of boots."

"This true?"

Mafale avoided Theodor's eyes and did not answer. His expression confirmed his guilt.

There was a block of dungeons at the rear of the Palace and that was where they took Mafale. He stayed obstinately silent, refusing to answer questions from Theodor or Lajeba. He was apparently too loyal to his unknown master. Or too frightened of him.

"Who told you to do it?"

No answer.

"Why did you do it?"

No answer.

"Where did you get the other boots?"

Still no answer. And so it went on. Now it was nearly five o'clock. Another half-hour and the Palace would be starting to bustle with life.

"Tie his hands and feet," said Theodor in exasperation. "And bring back that man Banwe."

Banwe was now apprehensive again, fearful about having been summoned to the dungeon, but his swagger began to return when Theodor gave him Lajeba's knife.

"This man refuses to talk," said Theodor. "If he does not talk I cannot know that he is guilty and then the blame will still be with you. So make him talk."

"He will talk, honoured sir," promised Banwe

grimly. "There will be no blame for me. He will tell you what you want him to tell you."

There were just the four of them in the dungeon—Theodor, Lajeba, Banwe and the defiant Mafale.

"You heard that," said Theodor to Mafale. "You will answer my questions or this man will hurt you very badly. Now—who gave you your orders?"

Still Mafale stayed silent.

Banwe approached him threateningly. "Answer the honoured sir."

Mafale spat at him. "Pig!" That single word was the first Mafale had spoken and it was obvious he had no intention of saying more.

Banwe used his sleeve to wipe the spittle from his cheek. He looked hard at Mafale, as if deliberating what he should do. And then, with a swift and deft movement, he flicked at Mafale with the knife. There was a thin stream of spurting blood and Mafale screamed as the severed lobe of his right ear fell to his shoulder and then down to the floor.

Banwe pressed the blade against Mafale's sweating face. "That was just a piece of an ear," he mocked. "A piece of an ear is nothing." His voice hardened. "Who gave you your orders? Tell the honoured sir."

Mafale stared past him at the wall, appearing not to have heard. Banwe seized the bed coverlet at Mafale's neck and ripped it away.

Now Mafale was again naked, with his hands secured behind his back. His head was still erect.

"No, a piece of an ear is nothing," said Banwe reflectively. "Perhaps this time we should try a different piece . . ."

"No . . . please, no," begged Mafale.

"Then tell the honoured sir."

And, finally, Mafale was broken by his terror of the knife and he told all he knew. He had been warned, when given his orders, that he would be killed if he ever talked. But now he was babbling out the facts.

"He told me it was because of his love and admiration for the President . . . they wear the same size in boots, you see . . . and he thought it would be a wonderful proud thing to stand in the boots of the President. There was no harm meant . . . it was just to be for the parade . . . it was just because of his love . . ."

Mafale, it was clear to Theodor, knew nothing about the poison in the heel. It was best left that way. Neither Mafale nor Banwe should know. Only Theodor and Lajeba knew that another attempt to kill the President had been narrowly thwarted—an attempt made by Major Anthanasius Ogwal.

They took the knife from Banwe and they untied Mafale. Then they left them together in the dungeon. "You will both be released after the parade," Theodor told them as he was leaving. Then, speaking to Mafale, he added: "If you wish to thank this man properly for your missing piece of ear, I will have absolutely no objection."

"Why?" asked Lajeba as he locked the door. "Why did you tell him that?"

"Because Banwe is a sadistic coward," said Theodor. "He's the sort of man I despise."

It took only a few minutes with polish to disguise the knife-mark in Amin's left boot. Then, just as his watch was showing five-thirty, Theodor removed the boots standing outside Ogwal's door. And he replaced them with those which had been intended for Amin.

He felt a little sorry for Ogwal, just as he had felt some sympathy for Moloro. But he knew that a man like Ogwal would certainly try again and so, for the sake of the Sanity International operation, there was no alternative. Ogwal had to die.

*   *   *

Theodor decided against trying to snatch an hour's sleep. It was tempting, very tempting, but he knew it would leave him with a cotton-wool head.

He lay on his bed for a while and he thought. What a terrible, messy confusion the whole business had become. Lives were beginning to seem as unimportant as candle-flames. In this mad and evil world men were no longer human-beings with hopes and dreams and aspirations. They were cardboard shapes, that was all. Shapes to be shuffled and manipulated and, if necessary, destroyed. There might, of course, be some to mourn them. Widows, perhaps. Or lovers or children. But the mourners were all cardboard shapes as well and so they didn't matter.

He was responsible, already, for the killing of Moloro who had been so loyal to Amin. Now he was to be responsible for the killing of Moloro's chief executioner, for exactly the opposite reason. They worried him, these thoughts. He tried not to let them but they still worried him. How many more were there to be? Dear God, how many more?

He felt better after a shower and a shave. A light breakfast. Just coffee and rolls. And then he was ready for his audience with Amin.

"I have often heard, Mr. President, of how you have the power to converse with the spirits of the dead."

Amin, his face impassive, nodded acknowledgement. "I am the favoured son of the Muzimu."

"Yes, the Muzimu," said Theodor. "Mr. President, I have to tell you of a strange dream which came to me in the night."

"You have permission," said Amin. "Continue."

"Is it possible—may I ask, Mr. President—for the Muzimu to speak through the dreams of those who served you with loyalty?"

"That is possible."

"Then last night I was indeed visited by the Muzimu. They came to me in my sleep and they brought me messages of warning and of reassurance. They told me, Mr. President, of an evil man who, even at this moment, is here in the Palace—plotting, sir, against your life."

Amin seemed unperturbed. "Who is this man?" he asked calmly.

"That, I regret Mr. President, was not revealed to me. Their visitation was, I feel, intended as a sign—a sign of confidence in me for the future. They indicated that he was a man of big stature, a man of high rank, but they gave me no name."

"That would hardly seem to be a sign of confidence in you," said Amin.

"With the greatest of respect, Mr. President, I feel it is. For they went on to tell me that they will show us this evil man—whoever he is—in the most dramatic way today.

"They intend, they told me, to strike him dead."

"And why should they tell you this?"

"As a token, I believe Mr. President. They recognised that, as a mere white man, I did not fully understand the power of the Muzimu. So they decided to demonstrate their power to me. They wished to prove to me how important it is for me to put my trust completely in them so that, in your service, sir, I may be guided by them in the future."

"In the Palace there are many men of high rank," said Amin. "We must see which one of them—if any—dies suddenly today."

*   *   *

Barbra was just finishing dressing when her telephone rang. It was Pierre Rey. "I'm downstairs," he said. "How about having breakfast with me?"

On the telephone his French accent struck her as stronger and more unpleasant than usual. "That I would enjoy," she said cheerfully. "Just give me two minutes, please, and I'll be down."

They talked easy trivialities through the meal. About his flying experiences. About her university days in Warsaw. About anything and about nothing.

After the meal, as they were being served with more coffee, he said: "I had a bit of a surprise this morning. A letter from Marcel. You know, my brother. I can't think what's got into him. It's only—what?—a day or so since I had that postcard from him. And now a letter. It's not like him, writing like that. Quite out of character."

"Did he tell you anything interesting?"

"Eh?"

"In the letter, Pierre. Did he say anything interesting in the letter?"

"No—and that's what makes it even odder. It was really quite a pointless letter. No news in it at all."

"He's still in Cairo?"

"Yes, still there."

"Where's he staying? Which hotel?"

"Damned if I know. Why?"

"Just interested, that's all. Didn't it say on the letter?"

"I suppose so . . ." He pulled the letter from an inside pocket and unfolded it. "Ah, yes . . . here . . . the Hotel Gezi."

"There is no Hotel Gezi in Cairo," said Barbra flatly.

"What're you talking about? It says so here on the letter-heading."

He pushed the letter towards her but she ignored it. Her eyes, fixed on his, were hard and determined. "There is no Hotel Gezi in Cairo," she repeated.

"I'm sorry . . . I don't follow . . ."

"I suspect someone is playing a joke on you," she said. "You check. There is no Hotel Gezi."

He chuckled as he put the letter away. "It's all that diving," he said. "It can do things to your head."

"You check," she said again. And then she abruptly changed the subject. "You keep on inviting me to your bungalow," she said. "Is the invitation open for this evening?"

He stared at her, bemused but delighted. "It's permanently open," he said. "It's open for the whole night if you want it."

"Will you collect me from here?"

"With the greatest of pleasure."

"Good," she said. "And then we can talk about Cairo and the Hotel Gezi."

"Well . . . perhaps we could find something even more interesting to fill the time."

"Yes," she said quietly. "Perhaps we could."

CHAPTER 6

Theodor, just behind Amin on the parade ground, was watching uneasily as the jet fighters came scything low over the horizon. He should have checked, he was telling himself. He should have checked and double-checked. But now it was too late.

Stretched out in front of them, right across the vast expanse of tarmac, were the regiments of Uganda. They tended to march, these men, with a sloppy and loose-limbed lack of co-ordination—their rifles clutched awkwardly at conflicting angles. But when rigidly at attention, as they were now, they looked as impressive as the finest of disciplined guardsmen. The two military bands, one to the left of the men and the other to the right, were silent. They had put the swagger into the opening ceremonial procession, one leading and the second bolstering the centre, and now they were redundant until the great march-off. And across the far side, behind the troops, were the grim and hugely-brooding tanks.

Now the jets were almost above them. Their V-shaped formation was so symmetrical, and they were travelling with such superb precision, that they seemed curiously unreal. They could almost be paper cut-outs which had been pasted, just a fraction too close to each other, on a great sheet of gliding glass.

Suddenly, as if being jerked by herd instinct, they were banking sharply, rolling their wings in nudging unison, before beginning to climb almost vertically.

Then they all flipped over simultaneously and they were screaming down again straight out of the sun.

Theodor's anxiety increased. It was unforgivable, he was insisting to himself, that he had not thought of it before . . .

It had nearly happened, as he well knew, in Tripoli in June, 1975. The situation there had been so very similar. Gaddafi of Libya, on a great State occasion, was surrounded by senior members of the Revolutionary Command Council when the Mirage jets were dipping their wings in salute to him. Aircraft on ceremonial duties there, as in Uganda, carried no live ammunition. Yet one of those jets at Tripoli had still blasted off a rocket.

That attempt on Gaddafi's life, by no means the first, had failed. The rocket narrowly missed the rostrum . . . but eleven people in the harbour area were killed by the blast.

An extra plane, it was suggested at the time, had slipped unobserved into the flypast.

That, Theodor realised miserably, could so easily happen again. It could happen in Uganda. And, if it did, he would be responsible for he had been picked to protect Amin—picked by Amin and by Stanton. But then, of course, if it were to happen—if a rocket were to find its target—he would not be there to accept the blame. He would also be dead. That aspect of it, he was slightly surprised to realise, did not particularly concern him. He was not afraid of death. Of the pain of dying, perhaps, but not of death itself—particularly if it were instantaneous. He was, however, passionately concerned for the success of the Sanity International mission. Amin had to be killed but it was imperative for the killing to look like an accident . . .

The jets screamed past. They circuited the parade-ground twice more and then, in an amazingly short time, they were mere midges in the blue distance. The air display was over.

Lajeba, at Theodor's side, touched his arm. "Brilliant flying," he said.

Theodor nodded. "Most impressive."

"Earlier this morning, though, I was a bit nervous about it."

"Really?"

"Yes, I had an uneasy feeling. So I had every one of those planes—and the pilots—checked over thoroughly."

"Good," said Theodor. "I assumed you had."

Now it was time for the gallantry awards. Nine men from the front rank were marched to the saluting base to collect medals and congratulations from the President. He beamed fondly at each of them in turn. He told them they were great heroes and that he was proud of them. No mention was made, however, of the manner in which they had distinguished themselves in battle. They had, in fact, obeyed orders in the most commendable Ugandan manner—and unquestioningly shot a specially-selected group of their comrades. The victims had been tied up at the time but the ropes had later been cut away. Their deaths, it had been reported, had been the work of foreign terrorists.

All through the award-giving the President had remained seated—the men kneeling to receive their medals—but now he stood to await his official escort.

Major Anthanasius Ogwal was to accompany him, as he always did on these occasions, during his token inspection of the troops. The pattern was well-established. Amin, with Ogwal and the rest of his entourage, would move slowly along the front two rows. He would stop to chat briefly with some of the men, joking with them or complimenting them on their appearance. Then, after a cursory glance at the rest of the troops, he would return to his saluting base for the final march-past.

Theodor could see Ogwal waddling monstrously towards them. More Brobdingnagian than ever. All bulging and blubbery. Like a wallowing whale in a wild, sick sea. Every step was a breath-struggling effort, sending fresh spasms of agitation through those drooping, quivering jowls of jelly. And in Ogwal's eyes was shining the joy of anticipation.

In just a few minutes, Ogwal was thinking, it would all be over. His Most Exalted Excellency President Anthanasius Ogwal. He was already savouring the title. He would make changes, of course. Many changes. There were those who had opposed him or dared to contradict him in the past. They, naturally, would have to die immediately. And the others would be rooted out. There would be no feuding or opposition, not in the country of President Ogwal. He was now nearly at the saluting base.

Just a few minutes . . . that was all. Amin, when responding to his salute, would stamp his right foot on the tarmac in the best military manner. That was the most predictable thing about Amin. He could always be counted on to stamp in a military manner. He would stamp solidly and decisively. And the metal point would be hammered into his heel . . .

Ogwal had been savouring this moment for many weeks. He had been concentrating his extensive ingenuity into it. He had weighed all the facts . . . the best method . . . the best time.

When Amin dropped dead, as he would be doing within the next two minutes, only one man could possibly take automatic command. Himself. Anthanasius Ogwal.

He controlled the parades. He always had. The soldiers would instinctively obey him.

He would announce that President Amin, for whom he had had such love, had been murdered by the tall German infiltrator he had, unfortunately, been foolish enough to trust. He would then shoot the German, there in front of all of them, to show them the strength of his feelings . . . to demonstrate his respect for the dead Amin . . . to show them how he intended to deal in future with all the enemies of Uganda.

Now he was immediately in front of Amin. This, at last, was the moment. He would, he decided, step back so that Amin did not fall on him.

For a brief second of gloating triumph he looked the President full in the eyes. Then he stamped as he saluted and, even as the salute was being acknowledged, he felt the prick of pain in his foot.

The disbelief and then the awful realisation surged through him. So did the poison. His eyes rolled back, blank and hideously white, and he took one staggering pace towards Amin before crashing mountainously to the ground.

Not one of the soldiers moved. It looked to them as if Ogwal had merely fainted. They were not surprised. The heat of the sun and all that fat he was carrying . . .

Theodor stepped forward and, kneeling, tried Ogwal's pulse. "This man is dead," he said to Amin.

"A man of big stature," said Amin thoughtfully. "A man of high rank." He was leaning forward now and speaking softly so that only Theodor could hear. "Were they not the words of the Muzimu?"

"They were the words, Mr. President."

"Then here is the proof of the confidence which the Muzimu have placed in you. They approve of you. They approve of you as my protector. In future you will travel with me always. Wherever I go, you go too."

"Thank you, Mr. President," said Theodor. "That is a great honour."

Later, when they were alone, Theodor repeated the conversation to Lajeba. And Lajeba was horrified. "But the flight to the Island!" he said. "The death flight! You can't go with him on that or you'll die with him."

"Yes, that's a nasty one," agreed Theodor. "I'll have to meet it when it comes."

*   *   *

"Yes, this is Theodor speaking."

"It's me—Barbra," said the voice on the telephone. "I've just come off duty and I'm back at the hotel. Would you join me for a drink?"

"When?"

"In half an hour?"

"I'll be there." He replaced the receiver.

They found a quiet corner. It wasn't difficult. The Metropolitan seemed to be attracting fewer and fewer drinkers.

"Congratulations," she said. "On today."

"For what?"

"For Ogwal. That was you, wasn't it?"

"How did you know? They said heart attack on the radio."

"I guessed."

"Oh." He looked despondent and miserably pre-occupied.

"Cheer up," she said. "It was a success—a victory."

"He had three young children."

"And that disturbs you?"

"This morning they had a father and tonight they haven't got a father. Yes, that disturbs me."

"Then start believing the radio. A man as fat as that —he could have a heart attack at any time."

"All right. A heart attack." He was gloomily uncon-vinced. "Let's pretend to believe that."

She raised her glass. "We'll drink to believing," she said. "*Prosit*!"

He tried to manage a smile. "*Prosit*!"

"I'm meeting Pierre Rey tonight. At his bungalow."

"You want me there?"

She nodded. "The time is right."

"How much does he know?"

"Almost nothing. He may be puzzling a bit about

Cairo and the Hotel Gezi or, of course, he may think I was just talking crap."

"Crap?"

"It's an English expression. A colloquialism. It means that you are not telling the truth or that you are just talking silly."

"Why should he think you were talking crap?"

"Because of the way I told him. I wanted to start him thinking, that's all. I wanted it to be just a little familiar to him for when we start talking about it again tonight."

He finished his tomato-juice and ordered more drinks.

"What do you think of him? Will he agree?"

"He's greedy and selfish and he enjoys life. He doesn't want to die."

"You've talked, then, about death?"

"Only in general terms. Don't worry . . . he doesn't realise that we know about him and his kidneys."

"But he will agree?"

"He will. Especially with the bait of £100,000."

"What time are you going?"

"He's collecting me from here at eight."

"I'll give you ten minutes with him at the bungalow. Then I'll be there."

"I understand."

"Barbra . . ." He was strangely hesitant. Suddenly embarrassed and gauche. "Barbra, there are things I want to say to you . . . things I wanted to say a long time ago." Another awkward pause as he sought for the right words. "About what happened . . . you know, in the old days."

"You mean during the war."

"Yes, those days. They were terrible days. Disgraceful days . . ."

She rested a reassuring hand on his. "That was a long time ago, Karl," she said gently. "Those days are dead."

"Perhaps. But the memories of them—they're not dead. You see, I know what happened to you. Well, quite a lot of it anyway, and I can't forget it was my people, the Germans, who did it."

"Karl, please . . . that's all gone. Let it rest."

He shook his head dolefully. "The things that happened, the things I helped to happen . . . they were shameful."

"I was proud of my German father," said Barbra reflectively. "Wilhelm Rademacher. He was a fine man and I was proud of him. And I loved my German mother. They were both very good to me."

"You know I was in Poland? I was at a place called Torzeniec. They talked about it afterwards. The massacre of Torzeniec, that's what they called it."

"I have heard about what happened at Torzeniec. They burned the houses, didn't they?"

"We burned the houses." Theodor put heavy stress on the first word. "We burned the houses and we shot the people."

"And you shot many people?"

"No . . . not at Torzeniec. There was a woman with a baby, but I couldn't shoot her. I pointed the gun at her but I couldn't shoot. I could only shoot soldiers."

"There's no bitterness in me, Karl. Not towards ordinary, decent Germans, and you're one of them. Please try to understand. War does things to men. It makes them do things they don't want to do because they're frightened. They're frightened of being killed, perhaps, or they're just frightened of people knowing they're frightened. It does awful things to men. But it doesn't completely change them, not deep-down change them. Men, really, are what they are. You, Karl, are a good man and I'm proud to be working with you."

He squeezed her fingers gratefully. "Thank you. I should be back at the Palace now. I'll see you later then, at the bungalow."

Pierre Rey was all set for seduction. On the brief drive from Mengo Hill he was thinking of Barbra. Not as a person but as a shape. He was thinking of how she'd looked that first day at the pool. The black costume had been clinging wetly to her, emphasizing the generous cambers of her body. He was wondering what she'd be like without that costume . . . what she'd be like in bed. She seemed so prim sometimes. So full of prudity. But he'd met the type before and it had always ended with shared pillows.

He reached the Metropolitan ten minutes early and was pleased to find her waiting in the lobby.

On the way back to the bungalow he pointed out a small and derelict building. "Hardly looks like a shrine now, does it?" he said.

"What sort of shrine was it?"

"That's where the sacred fire used to burn. The *gombola* fire, they used to call it. It was only allowed to go out when a Kabaka died."

"Then what happened to it?"

"They lit it again, for the new Kabaka."

"It's sad, isn't it, to think of all the customs and traditions that have gone."

"Why sad?"

"Because they were so important to people and now they are nothing."

He swerved to avoid a pot-hole. It wasn't a proper road any more—just a narrow and untended track worming upwards between the walls of forbiddingly impenetrable trees. "Oh, I don't know. Most of them were rubbish. But there were plenty of them here, right here on this hill. The royal hill—that's what this used to be. Do you know, there used to be a man here who had the job of guarding the umbilical cord of the Kabaka. Can you just imagine that! He'd take this disgusting thing and keep it hidden in some secret place all the time the Kabaka ruled."

"But why?"

"Custom, tradition, superstition . . . call it what you like. The idea, apparently, was that a man's umbilical cord was really his twin. They were of the same flesh. So any harm done to the twin was done to the Kabaka himself. That's the sort of crazy theories they used to have."

"So Marcel is your umbilical cord."

He laughed. "I've thought of him as many things but, I must confess, I never thought of him like that before."

"Perhaps you should."

"And is that supposed to mean something?"

They were now climbing the final shoulder of hard-packed dirt before reaching the front verandah of the bungalow.

"Your life depends on him, doesn't it?"

He switched off the engine and turned angrily towards her. "What the hell are you talking about?"

"Your kidneys—that's what I'm talking about." Her eyes were steady, her voice was brutally level. "The operation in November—that's what I'm talking about."

"Who told you?"

"Shall we go inside? It's probably more comfortable."

He glared again but got out of the car without another word. He sauntered up the three rickety steps to the verandah and she followed. There were a couple of cane chairs, on either side of a table made from a sawn-down barrel, and he slumped into one. "Well—who told you?"

She walked past him to the other chair. "You're dying, Pierre, aren't you? If you don't get that transplant you're virtually dead."

He looked thoughtfully at the bushes beyond the track. A pair of grey parrots, as if self-conscious under his gaze, erupted neurotically from the greenery, their noisy wing-beats breaking the silence as they sought a new sanctuary in the distant acacias.

"All right, so you know," he said eventually. "I can't imagine how you know but you do. Not that it really makes any difference. I am getting the transplant. It's all arranged."

"I'm sorry Pierre, but that's not true, not any more. It's all been disarranged."

"You're talking like a fool."

"Did you do as I suggested? Did you check on the Hotel Gezi?"

"Of course not. What sort of stupidity is this?"

"Then take my word for it. There is no Hotel Gezi."

"But . . ."

"Check if you want to. And then ask yourself another question: why should your brother Marcel pretend to be at a hotel which doesn't exist?"

"So you tell me. I'm just lost."

She took a pinch of snuff before replying.

"Because he's not in Egypt, Pierre, and he didn't write that letter. He didn't send you that postcard either."

"Look, I don't understand this joke, but—"

"This is no joke, Pierre. It's your life we're talking about and that's no joke. Marcel is a prisoner. It doesn't matter where, but he's a prisoner. And, what's more, there's a very strong chance that he'll soon be executed."

He got to his feet. "Who are you?"

Before she could answer, they heard a car complaining its way up the rutted track.

"Somebody's coming," she said. "He'll explain it to you—much better than I could."

Theodor pulled up behind Pierre's car and nodded curtly as he joined them. He waved a thumb towards the bungalow. "Is anyone in there?"

"No," said Pierre. "We're alone."

"Good. We'll talk inside. It's better."

They talked for two hours and, after getting his initial outrage and shock, Pierre was astonished by the audacity of the plan. "But it can't work," he said. "It can't possibly. Everyone on that plane will die."

"Everyone, as I've already told you, except you and me," said Theodor. "Now your choice, as you can see, is quite clear. If you do as we ask you'll be given a lump sum of £100,000 and a guaranteed passage to any country you care to name. If you decide not to join us—well—Marcel dies. And that means you die."

"Not much of a choice, is it?"

"No choice at all, really. And let me give you one final thought. Should you be stupid enough to mention any of this to anyone . . . should anything go wrong with this operation . . . Marcel dies anyway. So you'd just be talking yourself to death."

"You'd die as well."

"Yes, and so would Barbra here. But it's different for us. We're not afraid of death."

"How can I be sure of the £100,000?"

"I can't give it to you in advance, if that's what you mean. However, you'll get it."

"But I can't be sure."

"No. There's only one thing you can be sure of, Monsieur Rey. The fact that, if you don't co-operate with us, you'll soon be dead."

Pierre shrugged his shoulders in resignation. "Then obviously I've got to do it. I still think it's madness, but I've just got to do it."

* * *

EDSON LAJEBA: So now I can look back and see things as they were and as they are. Bugambe village hasn't changed much, not in all the long years. It is a huddle of huts on the edge of the Mabira Forest in Buganda province—almost halfway between Kampala and Jinja. It is a place of colour. Of jacaranda and tulip trees. Of greens and blues and vermilion which, because of the tropical sun, have a more vivid flamboyance than can be seen in the countries of the north. It is also a place which, in its time, has known too much disease and poverty.

THE KILLING OF IDI AMIN

We are Basoga people, descendants of the great Kintu, as can be seen by the graves of our dead. They always face south, the tombs of the Basoga. That is in homage to Kintu who came from the south and who started our race in the loins of Nambi, the daughter of Gulu.

The village depends on the banana shamba which is margined by the barrier of the majestic teaks to the east and, just beyond the fiery red of the termite mounds, by the banks of elephant grass to the west.

Sometimes the village men catch crocodiles which can be turned into shoes and handbags for the ladies of Paris and New York. There is much money in crocodiles. Europeans hunt them at night with fast motorboats. They have powerful guns and powerful lamps and they shoot the beasts at point-blank range. And then they gaff them quickly before they can sink.

The men of Bugambe have no powerful lamps or guns. They have no motor-boats. But they have a method which is just as effective. Double-pointed iron barbs, big as the anchor for a small boat, are baited with fish or—if it is available—the flesh of a hippopotamus. These barbs, with sturdy lines attached, are left in the papyrus for the crocodile to find. He is a greedy beast, the crocodile, and he does not feel the barbs until they embed themselves in the wall of his belly. And then he is trapped. No matter how much he writhes and fights, he is a captive until he dies of his injuries. All the men have to do is haul him in.

My European friends tell me that this is cruel but my European friends do not understand Africa. They could not understand, for example, the ways in which headmen like my father are required to impose their authority for the good of the community. The punishments which, just occasionally, he had to order—they would denounce them as cruel. They could never understand that such things are necessary for people to live in harmony.

There was this man, I remember, whose name was

Ofumbi. At times he had terrible and uncontrollable lusts. And at those times no woman in the village—no wife, sister or daughter—was safe from molestation by Ofumbi. One night he raped three women. Two from our village and a half-mad widow—a scraggy, gap-toothed old woman—who lived alone by the Jinja road. The men caught him and wanted to kill him but my father stopped them. My father ordered the punishment which was to be accorded Ofumbi. And the men took Ofumbi into the dark, loamy depths of the shamba to do as my father said . . .

They stripped him of his clothing and they spread-eagled him on his back, pinioning his wrists and ankles. Then they applied a poultice of quick-lime to his genitals. There were no more rapings in the village of Bugambe.

My father took me to Jinja when I was a small boy. He took me on the cross-bar of his bicycle and I could hardly believe the sights that were to be seen there. The world of today-and-yesterday, the one we knew so well in Bugambe, was jowl-by-jowl with the world of today-and-tomorrow.

There was the chemist's store with its scented sprays and its mouth-washes and its bottles of antibiotics. And there, right near it, was the booth of the native doctor who was peddling his own medicines and make-you-well charms—fur-balls from the stomach of a lion, the humerus of a pelican, the skin of a python. And, white as leprosy, the skull of a vulture.

Everything was there for a man with money. Cameras and cars . . . wireless sets and trilby hats . . . porcupine quills and aphrodisiacs compounded from the dried testicles of a chamaeleon. Liver salts and aspirins to ease headaches . . . the scales of a dead ant-eater to dull the pangs of childbirth . . .

Jinja, I decided at the time, was the most exciting place in the world.

My father told me I was not to use my life like the

other boys in the village. I was his eldest son, the eldest son of the headman, and I was to be educated. I was to be educated, not just at the missionary school, but like the white men and the wealthy people who lived in the towns. And the men of Bugambe were sent after crocodiles more often with their iron barbs to earn money for my education. "For it is not enough for you to be educated in Uganda," said my father. "Not even at a fine place like Makerere. You must go to other countries to learn their wisdom, perhaps even to England, for you are my eldest son and that is my wish."

So, in the fullness of time, I went to Makerere which stands on one of the hills of Kampala and which is the finest university in all of East Africa. I made friends there. Many friends. And my finest friend, the one with whom I spent most of my free time, was Amit Patell. He was the son of a merchant at Tororo.

I moved on, helped by grants and by money from the dead crocodiles, to the University of London. And I lived in a flat with three other students in a district called Earls Court. One day, I knew, I would go back to Bugambe to take my rightful place as the headman of the village but that would not be until the death of my father. In the meantime there was so much to learn and so much to do. And in 1970, when I was twenty-four, my father was so proud when I was able to tell him I had been accepted into the diplomatic service of Uganda.

January, 1971. A time of rumours and of confusion. A time of mounting panic and of terror. President Milton Obote was in Singapore for a meeting of Commonwealth Premiers and Government House, where I was now working, was a cauldron of conflicting reports. We heard stories of assassination plans . . . of mutinies . . . of bloody revolution. We heard the stories denied . . . then distorted to be told again in a new form . . . and we did not know who or what to believe.

"Six hundred Anyanya guerrillas from southern

Sudan have already invaded Uganda. They are wild and savage men and their faces are hideous with ochre . . ."

"No . . . not six hundred . . . four thousand of them, at least. They are already entrenched at Bombo and now they are sweeping towards the capital. They are killing every living creature. Raping and burning and killing . . ."

"That is not correct. They have not come as invaders. They have come by invitation to help protect the people of Uganda . . ."

And that, it began to seem, was probably the nearest we were hearing to the truth. The Sudanese warriors were coming in buses and lorries supplied by a company partly-owned by Felix Onama. And Onama, as Uganda's Minister of Defence, would never be helping any invasion . . .

But who had invited these men into our country? And for what purpose? Nobody really seemed to know.

People kept mentioning the name of Idi Amin. But where was Amin? At a secret conference in Lwero, said some. Under arrest at Fort Portal, said others. But, again, nobody really seemed to know.

Then, suddenly, everyone knew. The whole world knew.

The Sudanese, aided by break-away factions in the Ugandan army, seized control of armouries and of prisons such as the one at Luzira. And, more important, they captured the headquarters of the Malire Mechanical Regiment in Kampala.

Malire was the country's only unit to be equipped with armour—including six World War Two Sherman tanks which, like the Usi sub-machine-guns which were later to be used by Amin's squads of terrorist thugs, had been a gift from Israel.

Then the streets were littered with corpses. And the Nile, in places, was red with blood.

On January 25 Idi Amin became President of Uganda.

Men I knew and respected were executed. Some because, in the past, they had been critical of Amin or enthusiastic about Obote. Some for no apparent reason.

A government minister called Bataringaya was ripped to pieces while still alive and his head was displayed on a spike at Mbarara. There were many heads on many spikes. And there were many more men who just disappeared.

Perhaps I was too junior, too unimportant, to be killed. I don't know for in those days of madness there was no logic. But, whatever the reason, I was left unharmed. I continued with my duties in Government House. And I tried to shut my mind against the evil.

September, 1972. Refugees at Entebbe Airport. Asian refugees. I saw the long and hopeless queues of them—being roughly searched by soldiers and being robbed of their rings and watches and remaining bits of money—as I moved towards the departure lounge. I was on my way to join the Ugandan High Commission in London.

And then, in that procession of despair, I saw a face I recognised. Amit Patell. My old friend from the days at Makerere. He and his family were carrying all their possessions in torn paper bags and all life had drained from their eyes. I wanted to go to him, to offer some comfort, but I was afraid of the watchful soldiers. And so I pretended not to see my friend Amit and I caught my flight.

I have never seen him since. His people were among those herded on to a different plane which was bound for a different airport in England. I have often tried to comfort myself with the belief that perhaps he didn't see me. But I know, really, that he did. He knows that, in my fear, I rejected him. I was well-dressed and well-groomed and well-respected and I didn't even nod to him in his misery. That thought still makes me feel guilty.

It is dangerous for a Ugandan to talk freely about

the Amin regime. Even in London it is dangerous. But when one is with an old and trusted friend . . .

I met, quite by chance, this friend who had been studying with me at the University of London and he invited me to dinner at his home. We talked long into the night. We talked about the repression and about the brutalities. We talked about Amit Patell. And, eventually, he said I should meet another of his friends—an American who was on a visit to London. The American's name was Stanton.

* * *

The man called Nikodemo had a spoon. That was all. Just a spoon. He had managed to steal it without the guards seeing and he treasured it jealously. The six other prisoners in his cell at Makindye—all, like Nikodemo, on the waiting lists for execution—thought he was mad.

Hoping to escape from a place like Makindye armed with a spoon . . . that, surely, was madness.

They had been transferred together, these men, from the dungeons below the Central Police Station in Kampala. They had been transferred to take their places in the queue for death. They did not know when their turn would come. In a day perhaps. Or two days. It might even be a month or longer. But it would come. That was the one thing which was certain. Men never escaped from Makindye.

Yet here was Nikodemo with his spoon and his mad, impossible dreams . . .

Through the nights, working silently and in the darkness, he would scrape away at the concrete channels between the bricks of the cell. And always, before morning, he would mix the crumbled dust with his spittle—moulding it into a paste—and carefully press it back into place.

There was never anything to show, in the mornings, that Nikodemo had been at work. Night after night he persisted. Scraping and pressing back. More scraping and more pressing back.

Then he told his friend Rukidi and the others that the time had arrived. And they still thought he was mad and so he showed them. He showed them how easily one of the bricks could be eased out of the wall. Then the brick next to it . . .

Soon there was a hole big enough for a man to squeeze through. Rukidi was the thinnest and so he was chosen to go. It was right near the ground, the hole, and he wriggled through on his stomach. The jagged edges of the brick corset gripped him and tore gashes along his body. He wriggled painfully and furtively, helped by the desperation for freedom and by the lubrication of his own sweat.

Now he was in a sort of covered alley. There were rows of cells, all locked and identical, on either side of him. But there was no sign of a guard. He waited, his heart hurting with fear, expecting to be cut down by bullets from an unseen gun. But there was nothing . . .

Two huge bolts were fixed to the outside of each cell door and, stealthily, Rukidi slid them across to release Nikodemo and the others.

"Quietly now," whispered Nikodemo. He indicated the other cells. "Open all of them."

Soon there were fifty or more men in the alley. They were bemused, most of them, by this miracle. They had been waiting for death and now, unbelievably, they were being released. But still, intuitively, they kept the silence, moving fast like bare-footed phantoms through the uncertain shadows. And still there was no guard.

The last cell door was unbolted. "Follow me," whispered Nikodemo authoritatively. "This way . . ."

It was then that the guard, still frowsy with sleep, came around the corner. He was young and inexperienced and, startled by the sight of the uncaged men, he hesitated. He should have jerked the gun from his shoulder and screamed for help. But he hesitated. That hesitation cost him his life.

Four of them were on him almost instantly. They sprang, silent and ferociously as fighting cats. A hand was clamped over his mouth to stifle any shouts. And there were just feeble gurglings of protest, like water dregging down some distant sink, as they strangled him. Then, after taking his gun, they lowered his body delicately, tenderly almost, into the open sewer which ran the length of the alley.

There was a second guard with a machine-gun in the next alley. They shot him before he even saw them. And, working at feverish speed, they unlocked more and more cells.

Now there were a hundred men rampaging through the prison and each newly-opened door was swelling their numbers. They were no longer silent. They were jubilant and jabbering. All the tensions and the terrors . . . all the despair of their death-cells . . . they were all now exploding away in this cataclysmic geyser of relief. They were no longer men, no longer individuals. They were a berserk and frenzied pack, lusting for liberty and the blood of their tormentors. They surged forward together, amuck in a mindless paroxysm of hatred and pent-up violence. That one explosion from the gun, reverberating through the corridors of stone, had brought more guards. They were standing shoulder-to-shoulder firing wildly now, desperately and indiscriminately, into the horrifying advancing avalanche of hate. They killed and killed again. But still the pack surged forward and, slowly, they were forced to retreat. Some stumbled backwards in their fear, dropping the weapons as they scrabbled to save themselves. And the guns became the guns of the mob.

Rukidi dropped with a bullet in his brain. He was

alive. He could still see and hear and feel. He could still speak but there was no longer movement in his limbs. He was paralysed. He lay helplessly in the filth and the fresh blood and still, all around him and over him, the packed surged forward.

"Help me, please help me," pleaded Rukidi. But, with all the firing and the screaming and the yelling for vengeance, there was no-one to hear him, no-one to care. He was just another contorted mound, just another dead and useless man, and, in their freedom-scenting fury, they trampled over him with their heavy, bare feet. "Please . . . please help me . . ." But they were all gone now. The alley was unnaturally quiet. They were scrambling and fighting nearer to the barbed wire of the perimeter. They were killing and being killed. The shouting and the gunfire was away in the distance and around Rukidi there was little movement. Only the convulsive twitchings of men who would never stand again. Only the whimperings and the groanings and the throat-rattlings of death.

Thirty-seven prisoners died that day. So did eight of the guards. The other prisoners, eventually, were herded back into the cells. All except for five of them. Those five, two of them injured, did manage to escape. One of the three unharmed was the man called Nikodemo.

He stole a bicycle. He travelled alone and he travelled fast. He used the tracks he had discovered as a boy, the secret animal-carved tracks through the high-grass savanna, and by nightfall he was back in the hidden hide-out of his old FRONASA friends.

That was where he saw the newspaper. There were pictures in it of the great parade, the parade at which Ogwal had died.

"This man here," he said, stabbing his finger at a picture. "This man with the President. I've seen him before. Who is he?"

"That's the German," explained one of the friends. "His name's Theodor and he's in charge of State security."

Nikodemo scratched his head in puzzlement. "But that is not possible. He was a prisoner, this man. I actually shared a cell with him. Rukidi and me—we were with him in a cell at the police station in Kampala."

"He is the head of State security," insisted the friend.

"But it *was* him. I am sure it was him. There was him and an American who was sick . . ."

"Then, Nikodemo my friend, he was not there as a prisoner. He must have been there as a spy."

"A spy?"

"To listen, of course, to men like you and Rukidi. To learn, perhaps, about us and the organisation."

"But we said nothing. We did not even speak."

"No, but perhaps there are others who would not be so discreet."

"Now I remember . . . there was something strange about this man, about the way he talked. A doctor came to see the sick American and this man, this Theodor, was babbling strangely at him. He was trying to tell him of some plot to kill the President. He was there in prison—an enemy of the State, an enemy of the President—trying to talk of some plot to kill the President! The doctor, and now I recall it clearly, was refusing to pay any attention to him. He thought he was raving, that being in prison had turned his brain. And that is what I thought as well.

"Now wait . . . let me think. There was someone he kept asking for, someone he wanted to help him. Lajeba! Yes, that was the name. Someone called Lajeba!"

The friend pointed at the picture. "That one there is Lajeba," he said. "The one by his side. He is also an important man in State security."

Nikodemo pursed his lips in thought. "Then this Theodor must be taught not to play such terrible and dangerous games," he said slowly. "He—and the State—must realise that we cannot be fooled in this manner. There is only one penalty for spying."

"You are right," said the friend.

"Then it is settled," said Nikodemo. "This Theodor will die."

*   *   *

Nikodemo also had his spies. They were dedicated to the FRONASA cause and their information was usually reliable. That is why he was hiding in the clump of bushes on the edge of the Kampala-Jinja road. He was alert and watchful. And he was nursing a high-velocity rifle.

Lajeba was driving, with Theodor in the passenger seat beside him. They had left the Palace early in the morning and they were on their way to Jinja to vet security arrangements. This, Theodor considered, was of the greatest importance. The President was to make an official visit to Jinja and there had been many recent reports of guerrilla activity in the area.

"That's where my village is," said Lajeba.

Theodor was pre-occupied. "Sorry?"

"Bugambe. The village where I was born. You can't see it from the road but it's just over there."

"Is that so? I'd be interested in seeing it. Maybe we can call there on the way back."

"I'd like that. I'd be proud to introduce you to my father."

"Thank you. Then that's just what we'll do."

So they went on chatting, comfortably and easily like the good friends they had become . . .

Nikodemo could hear a car somewhere in the distance. He moved his rifle to the ready. He pulled open a small gap in the bushes and peered through but still he could see nothing. The road was completely deserted.

"About Pierre Rey," said Lajeba. "You're really confident about him, aren't you?"

"Never been more confident about anything. He'll do exactly as he's told. If only you could have seen his face when Barbra and I were talking to him at the bungalow."

Lajeba grinned. "Yes, I wish I could have been there."

Theodor laughed at the recollection . . .

Now Nikodemo could see the car. A small Peugeot. He lined it into his sights and he smiled as his finger curled loosely around the trigger. They were still too far away but soon they would be almost level with him . . .

"I'm still worried about you, though," said Lajeba. "That new ruling by the President—about you travelling everywhere with him."

"We'll work out something." Theodor did not sound convincing.

"But he'll insist, now, on you being on that aeroplane. And, if you do go, you won't stand a chance. You'll die with all the others."

"Forget it," said Theodor. "We'll work out something."

But both of them knew the size of the problem and there was an uneasy silence between them . . .

They were, Nikodemo estimated, now fifty yards away. His rifle was aimed squarely at the head of the big German and he was holding his breath in anticipation. Just one tiny squeeze and the man would be dead . . .

"There's something else here I meant to talk to you about," said Theodor. He leaned back suddenly to reach his document case on the back seat and, at exactly that moment, Nikodemo fired. The bullet flew through the open window, barely two inches in front of Theodor's face. Then it crunched into Lajeba, just below his ear, and he collapsed on to the wheel.

Lajeba's legs had spasmed rigidly straight and, unconscious, he was jamming down the accelerator. The car was surging like a suddenly-demented stallion and veering violently across the road. Theodor glimpsed the bushes, and the line of giant trees beyond, hurtling towards them. He grabbed at the wheel, shoving Lajeba heavily against the far door. A second bullet shattered a side window at the back. Theodor wrenched frantically at the wheel and, tires screeching, they broadsided into the bushes. The impact jolted Lajeba upright. For fifteen yards, half on the road and half on the verge, they scraped along the bushes and then Lajeba sagged heavily across Theodor's arms. Theodor lost any semblance of control and, again, they were roaring almost diagonally across the road. A third bullet hit the bodywork as they careered madly over the low bank at the far side and down into the tangle of untidy bushes.

Now they were bucking and juddering over rough ground and, with Lajeba's foot lighter on the accelerator, their speed was reduced. Theodor managed to weave an erratic passage between the bushes before, about a hundred yards from the road, they crashed into a young tree. The engine stalled. And, for the first time, Theodor realised that Lajeba was dead.

He got out of the car and, anticipating another attack, crouched behind the bonnet. But there was nothing. No more bullets. No sign of other life.

Lajeba's body was heavy and awkward to move. It was a struggle for Theodor to pull it across into the passenger seat.

The car, to his surprise, fired back into life without any trouble and, driving cautiously along a different route, he headed back towards the road. The point at which he reached the road was nearly a quarter of a mile on the Jinja side of where the shooting had taken place. There was no-one to be seen.

At Jinja he arranged for Lajeba's body to be taken back to Kampala. And, although he knew it was a futile gesture, he gave orders for a detachment of troops to be sent in search of the killer.

He went back to the Palace, eventually, with a guard of seven armed men. But, without Lajeba, he felt so desperately alone.

CHAPTER 7

There was a tranquillity and a dignity about Lajeba's father. He was a man who, despite the quiet courtesy of his manner, commanded respect and obedience. No stranger could possibly have guessed his age for his long, gherkin-shaped features had been cast in an ancient and timeless mould. He could have seen fifty summers . . . or sixty . . . or even seventy. He gave the impression of being untouched, and untouchable, by the years.

His wise, moist-brown eyes were recessed deeply in a dark face as crevassed as the bark of the forest trees and he had a grey-white beard of fine and wispy hair.

Tail-feathers from a cockerel, a symbol of his rank, jutted proudly from his skull-cap of brightly-daubed clay and a cape of baboon-skins was fastened loosely around his neck. It was an impressive cape which hung down his back like the gown of some Western academic.

Now he and Theodor were sitting alone on small stools.

"It was kind of you to come yourself with the news," he said. "I realise you have much to do."

"There is much to be done," agreed Theodor. "But he was my friend . . ." He stared at the dust, hating this duty he had given himself. "He was going to bring me here, you know. The day it happened . . . he was going to bring me here to introduce me to you."

"He told me much about you. He had much respect

for you, Herr Theodor. He said you were a good and honest man."

"Thank you for telling me. It was a mutual respect. We were a good team and your son was one of the finest colleagues any man could ever have. I have made arrangements for him to be brought back here this afternoon. I imagine that is as you would wish . . ."

Lajeba's father nodded gravely. "He will be buried with his ancestors in the manner of the Basoga. Now . . . how can I help you, Herr Theodor?"

"Help me?" Theodor was puzzled by the question.

"You say there is much for you to do and you have lost the help of my son. Do you need another, perhaps, to take the place of Edson?"

"That is most generous of you."

"It is not generous. It is for the sake of my son. There are many men in this village, many strong and intelligent men. Edson died doing his duty. He would have wished for that duty to be completed."

"Thank you, but no . . . really no. There is nothing I need. Nobody else. I'll find someone in the Palace to help me."

"To help you protect the President?"

"Of course."

"But I'm not talking about protecting the President. I'm talking about the real work—the killing of the President."

This jolted Theodor. He glanced anxiously around to make certain no-one else was within hearing distance. Then he looked hard at the old man. "He told you about *that*?"

"You appear surprised. Is it not the custom in your country for a son to trust his father?"

"How much did he tell you?"

"Enough. He asked for my blessing before he agreed to join with that American."

"Stanton."

"Possibly. I cannot remember his name. It is not important."

"Then you do not disapprove . . ."

Lajeba's father slowly filled his long-stemmed pipe with tobacco from the little box strapped to his wrist. He frowned in concentration as he lit the pipe. It glowed and made sizzling noises, sending up puffs of aromatic smoke. "It is as I told you," he said eventually, "Edson asked for my blessing and, because of the evil being done in this country, I gave it. I was worried for his safety, of course, but I gave him my blessing because I knew that what he was doing was right. So I will now ask you again Herr Theodor. You were relying on my son and now my son is dead. Can I give any help . . . for his sake?"

Theodor hesitated. There was an idea—just half-formed at the moment—but he was not really sure.

"Edson would have wished it," persisted Lajeba's father. "He would have been disappointed if I had not made this offer. And he would have been just as disappointed if you refused it."

"Well . . ." said Theodor. "Could you arrange for one of your men to attack me, to hurt me really badly?"

Now it was the turn of the other man to be perplexed.

"Please don't ask me why," said Theodor. "Just trust me when I say it would be a service. More than just a service in fact. It could be the means of saving my life."

The old man sucked his pipe impassively. "How badly would you wish to be hurt?"

"Very badly. Perhaps a knife in the back to start with. Yes . . . yes . . . that would make a very good start. Say your man were to stab a knife into my left shoulder, just about here." He indicated the spot. "That would be high enough to miss my lung but the knife could still go deep enough to bring a lot of blood. Then . . . let me think now . . . yes, then, after I've fallen to the ground, he could start kicking me. He'd have to kick really hard, hard enough to fracture one of my legs."

The rhythm of the smoke-puffs from the pipe was unhurried. "And then what would he do?"

"Just run away—that's all. He'd leave me there on the ground and he'd just run away."

"This is a most strange request."

"Please don't ask me for a reason. Just accept my word for the fact that it is important. I'll give you the time and the place where I wish this to happen."

"I am not sure that this is help of which my son Edson would approve. To hurt you in such a manner . . ."

"If your son were alive, I'd have asked him to do it himself. And, believe me, he would have done it."

"Very well," said Lajeba's father. "If that is really what you wish."

*   *   *

RICHARD CARTER: There've been so many women now that I can't start to remember them all. It would be like some men trying to count how many times they've ever sneezed. Women in Holland . . . Mexico . . . Malta . . . and Hong Kong. Women in France . . . Canada . . . Yugoslavia . . . and Indo-Bloody-China. An exceptional brace of nipples in New York . . . a distinctively sensuous thigh movement in Rome . . . sometimes the odd details stick. But there's rarely a name or a face to go with them. Sometimes a bit of this girl gets confused with a bit of that girl and the result is probably better than either of the originals. But there were those, of course, who were landmarks and they are the ones you don't forget. Like, for example, the very first one. No matter how many come after, you never forget the first one . . .

My father was what they call "in property." That means he got far too much money for doing far too

*little work and we were able to live at Winchester,
Hampshire, in a big house with servants.*

*It was one of those servants—a girl called Renee—
who won first place in my memory bank.*

*It was in the winter of 1960 and I was home from
boarding school for the Christmas holidays. She was
about nineteen or twenty and that, to me, put her right
out of my league. I mean, she was old—seven, maybe
even eight, years older than me. When you're twelve
years old you can imagine yourself with a girl your
own age or perhaps a bit older. But not that much
older. At least, I couldn't.*

*My parents were away for a few days at a family
funeral in Norfolk and on the Saturday the other servants were all out. Then, somehow, it just happened.*

*This Renee fixed my tea, just like she'd often done
before, and, as she was tidying away afterwards, she
suddenly said: "It must get awfully lonely for you—
being down here on your own." It seemed out of character, her saying that, but I had to admit she was right.
It was lonely and it was bloody boring.*

*And that was when she asked if I'd like to listen to
records in her room. Just for company. There'd be no
harm in it and there'd be no need to tell my parents.*

*"Just give me time for a bath," she said. "I always
like a bath when I've finished my work."*

*And when I got to her room, right at the top of the
house, she was wearing a towelling robe and she'd
opened a bottle of my father's red wine.*

*The light from her table-lamp was pink and soft and
there was smooch music coming from her portable
record-player. It was all set for a thoroughly corny
seduction. I can see that now. But at the time it seemed
like accidental magic.*

*She poured us each a tumblerful of wine and, in my
nervousness, I knocked back nearly half of mine in
one gulp. She topped it up and knelt on the rug, warm-
ing herself by the gas fire. "Make yourself comfy," she*

said. "Relax a bit." She patted the rug in invitation and her robe yawned open, revealing the lower slopes of her breasts and her pinky sward of stomach. She clutched it back into place. "Oops, sorry," she said. "I must get them buttons fixed."

I could feel the tips of my ears starting to redden and I looked away quickly. I hadn't realised until then that she had nothing on underneath. But, of course, my embarrassment was mixed up with elation. And that was being pushed higher by the wine. I wanted to keep watching her just to see it happen again but I kept my eyes averted.

"Well, come on," she said. "I don't bite."

I put my glass down between us on the rug. "Not bad, is it, this wine," I said. The record clicked at the end of its run and another fell in its place.

"I like it," said Renee. The new record was even smoochier. "But then I like any wine," she said. "As long as it's sweet."

She reckoned the pink and soft light was too harsh so she switched it off and we sat by the glow of the fire. And we drank more wine.

"You smoke cigarettes?" she asked.

"Well . . . I have done. You know, at school. But my father says I'm not to."

"Then your father doesn't need to know, does he?"

She lit two cigarettes and gave one to me. Then she changed the records and, as she settled back on the rug, she gave me a coy sort of look. "You were peeping, weren't you?" she said. "You were peeping at my boobles."

"No . . . no I wasn't." I'd never heard them called that before.

"Yes you were. You were looking through the gap in my robe—seeing what you could see."

I remember protesting that I wasn't. It was really quite pathetic. Then I finished the wine, just to hide *my confusion, and I stared at the empty bottle as if it was the most fascinating thing in the world.*

"There's no need to peep, darling," she said. "If you want to have a look, have a look. There's no law against having a look."

Then she opened her wrap like a pair of curtains, draping it against the outside foothills of her breasts. Even after all these years, and so many others, I can remember them exactly as they were.

They were jutting out like a pair of challenges, the nipples baby-pink against the darker circles of their launching pads.

"Well—what do you think of them?" She seemed to be waiting for a round of applause.

"How do you mean?"

"My boobles. Do you like my boobles?"

I nodded. "They're lovely," I said.

She looked at me thoughtfully for a moment or two and then she said: "You haven't seen them before, have you? Not on any girl." She eased herself closer to me and she smelt good. "Well, have you?" she persisted. "Have you ever seen a girl with nothing on?"

Christ, but I was getting excited. Excited and frightened at the same time. I didn't have to answer her. She already knew. I think she'd known long before I'd stepped into her room. She took my fingers and guided them to her, pressing them to her lips and her chin, easing them down her neck and to the peak of her left breast. "There, that's better," she said. Her voice had gone all low and husky as if it had been filtered through fog. "That's what you wanted to do, isn't it?"

And suddenly there was an explosion inside me. I remember lunging forward, my arm going round her and my lips wet against her face. And with my other hand I was squeezing at her breast. She started half-

moaning: "Oh, darling . . . oh, my innocent little dar-
ling . . ."

Then, unexpected, she pushed me away from her
and squirmed clear. She squatted about a yard from
me and, for a moment or so, I was puzzled and angered
by this apparent rejection. I didn't know what to say
or do and then she broke the silence. "You'd better get
those trousers off," she said. "Or you're going to burst
out of them."

And still, like an idiot, I didn't react. She leaned
forward to unfasten my leather belt and her experienced
fingers, undoing my fly, brushed against my firmness.
She saw what that did to me and, before I could grab
her, she leapt to her feet, wriggling out of the robe and
letting it fall in a heap. She backed away a couple of
paces, her eyes glistening with excitement and her arms
open to me in invitation. I don't know how long I stood
there. In the flicker of the gas-fire she looked like all
the naked women I'd imagined but never seen. She was
smooth and firm and perfect, though her triangle of
down was fairer than I'd expected—lightish-brown with
highlights of gold.

"Come on, darling," she said. "Come and see if it's
as good as it looks . . ."

Another bed . . . another girl . . . another landmark.
Your first taste of adultery . . . the first time you have
another man's wife . . . that's another thing you don't
forget.

I was twenty then and her name was Magyar. Well,
it was Margaret really—or Maggie for short—but she
called herself Magyar because she was a model and
thought it sounded classier. She had huge sea-green
eyes and jet-black hair and I met her at a party in
London. After two drinks she was helpfully telling me
that she lived all on her own . . .

We got back to her place about two in the morning
and, as she closed the front door, she said: "Cigarette
and drink first? Or do we go straight to bed?"

She noticed my look of surprise and smiled. "We both know what it's about," she said. "So why waste time?" She let her dress slide from her as she led the way to a bedroom at the back. "Undo me, will you." I released the hooks of her bra and felt it go slack. She shook her shoulders and let it fall to the carpet, her back still towards me. My arms were around her then and her nipples were as fat and hard as my smallest fingers. My hand moved down the sleek undercliff of her stomach and slipped beneath the elastic barrier of her pants. She shuddered closer against me and moved her legs to trap my leading finger. It was locked in the warm softness.

"Jesus, but you're lovely," I said.

She gave a small laugh of pleasure and wriggled free. "You really think so?" She flung the pants away and they landed across the top of the dressing-table mirror. She was facing me now, posing theatrically. "You really do think so?"

"Bloody fantastic!"

She threw herself on the bed, her arms and legs spread like four spokes of a wheel. "That's what I get paid for," she said. "Looking lovely. It's my career."

I started to loosen my tie and moved towards the bed but she sat up quickly and perched on the pillows. "No! You mustn't touch me—not yet. I like to see what I'm getting."

"Eh?"

"Your clothes, Dickie love, your clothes. I want to see you without your clothes. It's strip-tease time and I'm going to sit right here watching."

I was down to my pants when she threw her legs over the side of the bed. "Let me do that," she said quickly. "Let me unveil it."

She was like a little child feeling a birthday present before taking off the wrapping. Stretching out the moment. Savouring the agony of anticipation. And I was worried that the anticipation would be too pro-longed for me . . .

Her nails were deep in my back as I crested the long surge and I could feel the marks of her teeth on my shoulder.

"Like that cigarette now?" she asked eventually.

But this was no time for cigarettes. I wanted her again while she was warm and damp beneath me. And her thighs began to throb and the cigarettes were forgotten. And, afterwards, I couldn't remember ever having felt so exhausted before.

There was only one cigarette in my pocket.

"I've got some," said Magyar. "Over in that drawer."

I went to the drawer and saw that, under the packet, was a heap of men's things. Vests, pants, socks. That sort of thing. I fished some of them out and held them up. "Who the hell do these belong to?"

"Oh, those," said Magyar lazily. "They're my husband's."

Christ! I'd never messed with a married woman before. "You said you didn't have one," I said.

"Dickie love. I said I was living alone tonight. That's all I said."

"Then where is he?"

She yawned. "Birmingham, I think. Or is it Coventry? Somewhere like that."

Suddenly I was very conscious of my nakedness. It was her being married that did it. I pulled on my pants and she frowned with disappointment. "Why?" she asked. "You've got a nice thing. There's no need to cover your thing."

My thing, as she called it, had now shrunk with anxiety. As if iced water had been poured over it. I was already imagining myself being named in the divorce.

"Your husband—when's he coming back?"

"Monday. He's at a conference."

"And what does he do?"

"Anything in skirts," said Magyar.

After that night it never mattered. Single . . . married . . . what the hell! Why feel guilty about husbands? They were probably doing the same in Birmingham or Coventry or wherever. And if they weren't—well, hard bloody luck.

I suppose, in a way, the girl from the convent should have been a landmark. After all, it was through her that I got kicked out of school. But I can't think of her that way. She was just a ten-minute tussle behind the cricket pavilion. I got mud on my knees and she bitched because I tore her blouse. Stupid little bag.

But really, of course, she did make a hell of a difference to my life. Changed it completely in fact. It was all fixed for me to become something solid and respectable—a lawyer, perhaps, or even a barrister. Being chucked out of school put the cap on that.

I pushed off to sea. I didn't tell my parents or anyone. I just scraped together all the cash I could and I pushed off.

Deck-hand on a cargo-boat. Run there . . . lift this . . . scrub that . . . and spew your ring up twice a day. It was bloody and I jumped ship in Buenos Aires. And after that I started living on my wits—renting myself out to the highest bidder.

You get a sort of word-of-mouth reputation after a while and you'd hardly credit some of the work I've handled. But I've never given a damn, not if the money was right. There was, for instance, a millionaire in Bermuda who wanted a disposal job done. His wife's lover had to get the big chop. Funny when you think about it, isn't it—a jealous husband turning to me for help.

I chopped the lover all right and I fed him to the fishes. The millionaire paid up handsomely for that one. I wonder what he'd have said if he'd known I'd been knocking off his wife at the same time.

It was after the Bermuda job that I got a telephone call from this American. He said his name was Stanton.

*   *   *

Cherif the Moroccan was worried. "When this business is over I wish to go to Tangier," he was saying. "I wish to go there with the money and buy myself a big and beautiful shop."

"Great idea," said Weaver casually. "With some big and beautiful birds to help you, I suppose. Just your line, that is. You'll make a bloody fortune."

"But I am frightened that perhaps it will not be that way."

"Course it will. God, you're a natural. I can see you there right now. A load of leather tat . . . conning all hell out of the tourists. Oh yes, you'll make a fortune all right."

"No. I am thinking now that perhaps the police will come. They'll come for you and for me and there'll be no shop. Only prison, perhaps."

"Aw, knock it off, will you? Why the hell should they come looking for us? They don't even know us. They haven't got a clue who we are."

"They might trace us through the Englishman."

"Carter? And what makes you think they'd find him?"

"Because the woman knows his name. His real name."

"Jesus! No!"

"Yes, she knows and they will find him. They will question him and, in the end, he would lead them to us."

"You certain about this?"

"My cousin heard them talking. He was sitting just over there and he could hear them. The woman had seen the Englishman's driving licence."

"Christ Almighty! But that would have his address and everything on it!"

"She found it in the pocket of his trousers."

"The stupid, randy twat! I told him to keep away from her. Time and again I bloody told him. Now he's really ballsed it up."

"My cousin didn't tell me right away. He didn't understand how important it was."

"Well, let's be glad he bloody told you in the end."

"Perhaps it would be stupid, now, to let her go free?"

"I don't know. I just don't know."

"Nobody knows she and her husband are here. Nobody knows they're even in Morocco."

"You suggesting we kill them?"

"There would be no risk. No-one would come looking."

"Let me think about it," said Weaver. "I've just got to think."

*　　*　　*

"Stanton's sources of information are quite incredible, aren't they?" said Theodor. "So is his sense of timing."

It was dark. He and Barbra were driving up the track to the bungalow on Mengo Hill where Pierre Rey was waiting for them.

"You have learned something new?"

"Enough to make me appreciate just how accurate Stanton was. This secret visit of Amin's to Pemba Island—it's one of the key parts of the final build-up to total war.

"He's got meetings lined up there with terrorist leaders—anti-white fanatics, the lot of them—from all over. It seems certain they're now ready to pledge the support he needs. And, if that is the situation, he'll be ready to press the button. Bang—straight into Rhodesia and South Africa."

"So it's just as well then, isn't it, that he'll be dying on that flight?" said Barbra. "This island—where exactly is it?"

"Indian Ocean, south of Mombasa," said Theodor. "About seven hundred miles or so from here."

"An easy straight flight then. His Citation's got a range of nearly fourteen hundred miles."

"Will you have any problems fitting the stuff into it?"

"None that I can visualise. It's got one of those drop-out constant-flow oxygen systems for emergency use and that's going to make it very simple. No, there'll be no problems—as long as I have enough time to work undisturbed on it."

"You'll have the time. I'll see to that."

They were now at the bungalow where Pierre was waiting on the verandah. They followed him through to the living-room.

"Nobody saw you coming?"

"Security is my specialty," said Theodor. "Remember?"

"As long as you're sure. I don't fancy getting my head chopped off."

They took seats.

"A drink?"

Theodor declined. Barbra asked for a gin-and-tonic. Pierre fixed it and a whisky for himself.

"Now, let us go over the whole thing so that we're perfectly clear about exactly what will happen," said Theodor. "Everything on this flight will be normal, absolutely normal, until we're crossing over the coast. Then—you tell me. What is it you do?"

"Well, first of all I switch to autopilot—"

"That's the standard one, I presume," interrupted Barbra. "The Bendix FGS-70."

"That's the one. A good piece of engineering. I switch it on and then I flick on the gas. Look . . . I've been thinking about this. This gas stuff, what exactly is it?"

"You want the formula?" asked Theodor.

"Well, I'm not a chemist . . ."

"No, so it wouldn't mean much to you. Let's keep it simple. It's a variation, a very sophisticated variation, of the old VX nerve-gas."

"Wasn't that the stuff there was such a row about a few years ago? It killed a few thousand sheep, I seem to remember, in Utah. Somewhere in that area, anyway. And the American Army was supposed to have lost a couple of cylinders of it in a lake up in Alaska."

"A couple of hundred cylinders, actually," said Theodor. "They were surprisingly careless. But you're quite right. It is basically the same stuff. It comes from the same sort of organic-phosphorus compounds. But, as I said, it's far more sophisticated. You turn it on and it will come seeping through the oxygen drop-out system. It won't kill anybody, as I told you before. It will just paralyse them. Completely paralyse them. They'll be conscious, of course, but they won't be able to twitch a muscle."

"And that's when I put on the mask."

"That's when we *both* put on the masks," said Theodor. "And we do it quickly. I'll be with you in the cockpit and we'll have about thirty seconds."

"These masks—they are absolutely effective?"

"Completely. They couldn't possibly be safer. Nothing can get into them. They have an hour's air-supply—and that's far more than we'll be needing."

"Could I have one to do some tests on?"

"I assure you it's not necessary."

"I'd still feel happier."

"All right—then let's make you happy. What would you use for the testing?"

"I don't know yet. Smoke perhaps. Or any sort of fumes would do."

"I'll see you get one tomorrow," said Theodor. "And, once you're satisfied it is perfect—and I can promise you it will be—you might like to keep it locked away somewhere."

"I intend to," said Pierre. "I wouldn't want it switched."

"What a pleasantly suspicious mind you have," said Barbra.

"It's the company I keep, darling. Also, I'm one of nature's survivors."

"Let's get back to it," said Theodor. "The gas is now on and so are our masks. What do you do next?"

"Switch on the taped message."

"That's right . . . the Mayday message. And, while that's being transmitted to coastguards and shipping, we'll be busy baling out into the ocean. And we'll be doing it right at the spot where the boats will be waiting to pick us up."

"You have used a parachute before?"

"Many times," lied Theodor. "And we know you have. It's on your records."

"And the boats . . . they will be there, won't they? They will be in the proper position?"

"They will."

"Well, you've got to be completely sure of that, you know. It's a damn big ocean."

"Yes, and it's got some damned hungry fish. Don't worry . . . it's like I said before. There'll be a whole network of them. It's all organised, for my sake as well as yours. I don't fancy trying to swim ashore because drowning's not my idea of fun."

"And what about other vessels in the area? Say they see us coming down and pick us up. That would be bloody awkward, wouldn't it? There'd be me being dragged on to some strange boat while my voice would still be bleating away in the aircraft."

"It'll be dark, remember. That's how Amin wants it. It's the official plan for him to arrive after dusk so that his visit stays secret. There'll be no chance of anyone spotting us, not with our black parachutes. We'll just drift down like invisible ghosts."

"And our bleepers will bring the right boats straight to us."

"Absolutely," said Theodor. "Then they'll take us to a lonely spot on the mainland where there'll be an aircraft waiting."

"Then on to Switzerland together for the money."

"That's right. Geneva."

Pierre finished his whisky and poured another. He did not offer to replenish Barbra's glass. "I've got to admit . . . it's damned clever," he said. "And while we're being whisked ashore the old Citation will still be flying, further and further out into the Indian Ocean."

"Yes . . . with your voice still transmitting from the tape," said Theodor. "It'll seem that you're still up there in desperate trouble with your controls jammed. And eventually the plane will run out of fuel and just disappear under the waves. Just an accident. Nothing more. Just a terrible accident."

"What about the gas cylinders? Won't they be a bit bulky and obvious?"

"No," said Barbra. "You've got sixty cubic feet of baggage space in that plane—forty-three in the cabin and the rest in the nose. We'll fit the cylinders up front."

"And I'll be doing the pre-flight security search myself," said Theodor. "So there'll be no problem there."

Barbra ostentatiously took a pinch of snuff. "My glass is beginning to feel neglected," she said pointedly.

Pierre mumbled a vague apology and got her another gin-and-tonic.

"Thank you. There is one other matter," she said. "I've been thinking about the fuel. You'll be leaving Entebbe, presumably, with full tanks?"

"That's what I usually do. I would normally have topped up at Pemba before the return flight."

"Then I suggest you start jettisoning the fuel immediately after you've switched on the gas. There's no point in the plane flying on for a further seven hundred miles. A hundred or so will be enough."

Pierre nodded his understanding. "I'll see to that." He turned back to Theodor. "But don't forget, I want that mask. I want to be able to test it. Really thoroughly test it."

"I'll be back tomorrow night," said Theodor. "I'll bring it then."

* * *

On the high and desolate ridge, beyond the luxuriance of the banana shamba, a solitary tree stood high above the euphorbias and acacias. It had been ravaged, at some time, by lightning and most of its limbs were blackened and withered. It was dying there, in the place which men had dedicated to death. There were, however, clumps of greenery still clinging defiantly to some of its doomed branches and, in one of them, the old owl was liquidly chirruping his welcome to the twilight.

Fire-beetles danced phosphorescently in the nebulous distance. And all around was the unseen night choir of the full-bellied toads. The men had now all gone back to the village. They had filed back mournfully and in silence.

And around the grave of Lajeba there were only the creatures of the night. It faced south, that grave, like the others around it. For Lajeba was a descendant of the great Kintu. He was a Basoga.

* * *

Theodor handed Pierre Rey a package and an envelope. "The gas-mask," he said.

"And what's this in the envelope?"

"Your new passport. Take a look."

Pierre slit the envelope and found it contained a French passport bearing his photograph. The name in it, however, was "Henri Lefarge."

"What's all this about?"

"You're working with professionals," said Theodor. "You should realise that by now."

"So?"

"So it's obvious, isn't it. When that plane goes into the sea it's going to be news. Big news. The death of the President of Uganda. The reporters will be squeezing out every detail they can. For radio . . . television . . . newspapers . . . all over the world. And one of the facts they'll play up is the fact that your voice was heard almost until the end. In other words, you were on that plane and you died on that plane.

"Your local paper, back home in Corèze, will be bound to give you the full treatment. Local Man Dies in President's Death Plane. That sort of thing. Pierre Rey will be dead. Completely and irretrievably dead. So you could hardly come popping up again, could you? Not as yourself. Once we are pulled out of the sea you will be Henri Lefarge."

Pierre studied the passport. "I see. You've knocked two years off my age, I notice, and you've shifted my birthplace to just outside Marseilles. Who made up those details?"

"Nobody made them up. They happen to be true. All the details there, they match the real Henri Lefarge."

"So this is a copy of the trick used by that British Member of Parliament, then . . ."

"Not exactly. Stonehouse used the identity of dead men. Lefarge is very much alive."

"You have to pay him much?"

"He knows nothing about it and he never will. He's a very ordinary, not-too-bright farm-worker who has never been out of France and who is never likely to step out of France. He'll never need a passport."

"Then how?"

"Very simple. We applied for it in his name. We sent off his details and your pictures. And we had . . . what shall we call it . . . an understanding with the village postman. He should have delivered a certain official package to Lefarge. Instead, he got a small sum for diverting it to us. There was no risk in it for him, of course, because Lefarge wasn't expecting any package."

"Henri Lefarge, eh? That'll take some getting used to."

"A Henri Lefarge with £100,000 to spend as you please."

"Yes, well I suppose that makes up for being labelled an Henri. I can't say I like the name very much. What about you? What will your name be?"

The question was one for which Theodor was unprepared. "Oh . . . I won't need one," he said quickly.

"But you'll be in the same position, won't you? You'll be on the plane. Your name will get into the papers as well. Personal bodyguard to President Amin. Head of State security and all that. The German papers particularly—they're bound to print pictures of you and everything."

"They won't have any pictures, not of me," said Theodor.

"But, even so, they're certain to print what they can about you and your background. You were in the police force, weren't you, in Munich?"

Theodor was thinking fast. "No," he said. "Karl Theodor was, but I wasn't. I shall merely have to revert to my own name. My real one."

"Then you're not really Theodor?"

"Of course not. The name was picked for me—just like Lefarge was picked for you. I don't know Karl Theodor and I have no wish to. He'll die—officially, at any rate—in the crash. And if that creates any problems for some policeman in Munich—well, that's hardly my concern. I'll simply go back to being myself."

"And who are you really?"

"I came to Uganda as Theodor. I shall leave Uganda as Theodor. Let's leave it at that for the moment."

He pulled a transistorised tape-recorder from his inside jacket-pocket. "I thought this would also be a good opportunity to do the recording."

"The Mayday one?"

"What else? Here . . . I've written a script for you."

He handed Pierre the paper. "Now think of the position you're supposed to be in. You're in a plane that's out of control. Your steering's gone completely and your radio's faulty. You can transmit on it but you're not receiving anything. All right. You're trying to stay calm but, at the same time, there's this urgency and this feeling of panic growing inside you. We need to sense that. We need to hear it in your voice, in your inflections."

"I'm a pilot, you know, not an actor."

"Yes, you're a pilot. You're a pilot with kidney problems. Don't start forgetting those problems."

"What about Marcel and Yvette? What will happen to them afterwards?"

"What's this then? Suddenly being concerned about somebody else! That doesn't sound at all like you."

"I'm thinking of the operation, damn it. He will be released, won't he? He will be there for the operation."

"You may have to explain to him why he's giving his kidney to a man called Henri Lefarge."

"That's no problem, not with my brother. Just as long as he's there."

"He'll be freed in plenty of time," said Theodor solemnly. "That is something I can guarantee. Now, shall we get on with this recording?"

It took nearly three hours before Theodor was satisfied with the tape. Pierre's voice sounded too stilted. It lacked urgency and conviction. So they kept going over it, erasing and recording again, perfecting every nuance.

"Right," said Theodor eventually. "That will do fine."

He put the recorder and the tape in his pocket. "I'll keep these for the moment."

And, on the drive back to the Presidential Palace, he was satisfied with the work of the evening. Pierre, he told himself, was now well beyond the point of no return.

CHAPTER 8

"You will obey me and you will ask no questions," said Lajeba's father.

The young man standing respectfully before him was slightly-built but he was sinewy and strong. There was no expression betrayed on his face but he gave a small nod to signify his compliance.

"You will find the white man Theodor at the appointed time and at the appointed place. He is a friend, you will remember. He was a friend of my son and now I have given him my hand in friendship. That is why, if you do not wish to be punished, you will be careful not to hurt him more than is necessary."

He paused to light his pipe and the young man, head held high, waited attentively. Lajeba's father was no longer wearing his bright clay cap with the cockerel feathers. His hair was covered with a kerchief of plain white cotton. He was in mourning.

He looked at the young man for a few moments, his moist-brown eyes challenging, as if he was half-expecting a question or an objection. There was none and he went on: "If this man Theodor was to die because of your actions, or if he was to be hurt too severely, your own life would be held forfeit.

"He will be alone and you will approach him, as he has requested, from behind. You will stab him at the top of his left arm.

"He will be silent while you are attacking him. He will not shout and he will not resist. He will let you do what I am ordering you to do, for that is what he wishes. So . . . you will stab him at the top of his left arm and he will fall to the ground. Then you will kick him. You will kick him once in the face so that the flesh becomes bruised and ugly. You will kick at his legs until one of them is broken. Then you will run away."

The young man nodded again. "Do I then return to Bugambe?"

"No, you go to the west. There must be nothing to connect the attack with this village. You will go to the west and you will stay there for one month. Then, and not until then, you will return to Bugambe. Do you understand everything I have said?"

"I understand."

"Then go now. And be mindful of what I have told you. If the man Theodor dies, you will not return from the west. I will send men there to find you and they will kill you."

"I will return as you have ordered," said the young man. "After the passing of one month."

*   *   *

"I've changed my mind," said Pierre Rey. "I can't go through with it after all."

Theodor put down his tomato-juice and glowered at him. "What the devil are you talking about?"

"The whole scheme. It's much too risky . . . so many things could go wrong."

They were again in a corner of the Metropolitan bar. The staff had become accustomed to seeing them drinking together but, of course, that seemed perfectly natural. They were both white men who were highly-regarded by the President. They had so much in common.

"In that case you won't have to wait until you are killed by your kidneys," said Theodor viciously.

"And that means what?"

"Remember Moloro? You ought to. You were there

watching. Well, how would you like to go back to the Pit of Death? Eh? How would you fancy being the star attraction?" He continued quickly before Pierre could reply. "Ogwal's gone, of course, but there are still some interesting ideas about. The President was telling me last night that he has never seen an unarmed man fighting with a lion. That would be a treat for the crowds, wouldn't it? Particularly if it was a white man."

"That's crazy talk. The President trusts me. He wouldn't—"

"It would be quicker, I suppose, than waiting until your kidneys rot completely away," interrupted Theodor reflectively. "But it would be frightening, wouldn't it? Oh yes, and painful . . . and very messy . . ."

"I saved the President's life once." There was now uncertainty and a suggestion of fear in Pierre's voice. He was talking as if trying to convince himself. "I saved his life and he gave me an award for it. The Silver Ugandan Cross—that's what he gave me."

"He gave Moloro one of those Crosses. He also gave him the Simba Star for gallantry." He could see the effect of his words, but Pierre had to be more than frightened. He had to be petrified. So Theodor went on ruthlessly elaborating: "Yes . . . very messy indeed," he said. "But that need be no problem. We could, perhaps, later release a pack of hyenas there. They're wonderful, you know, for clearing away bits of carrion. And that's what you would be, Monsieur Rey. Just bits of carrion. They also eat bones and—"

"The President wouldn't allow me to be killed," insisted Pierre desperately.

"He wouldn't *allow it*! He'd *insist* on it . . . after I'd finished talking to him. I'd tell him about the plot I'd uncovered . . . the plot organised by you to kill him. I'd let him hear the tape, the one with you play-acting on. The panic in your voice—I think it might amuse him, and you know how he loves to be amused. I'd explain to him just what you planned to do and how you planned to do it."

"But—"

"Shut up and listen. Then I'd show him your Henri Lefarge passport. Oh yes, I didn't make the mistake of leaving it at your place."

"You are a bastard."

"No," said Theodor. "Just a realist. And it would pay you to be the same. The alternatives are very clear for you, aren't they? You can die here within the next few days, publicly and agonisingly. Or you can live a life of luxury anywhere in the world with £100,000 tax-free."

"When do I get the passport?"

"On the flight. I'll give it to you then. After the gas has been released. By the way, have you tested that mask yet?"

"No, but I'm going to."

"Good. That'll reassure you, and I do want you to be quite happy in your mind." Theodor raised his glass. "Happy landings," he said.

Pierre did test the mask. He locked himself in the bathroom of his bungalow and used towels to seal the cracks around the door. Then, with the mask ready, he dropped a handful of calcium carbide into the sink which was brimming with cold water. The small room was soon full of acrid acetylene fumes but, secure within the mask, he breathed without discomfort.

For fifteen minutes he stayed there. The test had to be good and thorough.

Finally, satisfied, he pulled the plug to release the contaminated water and opened the windows wide. Then he put an electric fan into the bathroom to speed the dispersal of the foul smell.

*   *   *

The night before take-off. "This conference at Pemba—it is a very important one, Mr. President?' asked Theodor.

"An understatement," said Amin brusquely. "It is the most important conference ever held in Africa. It's one that will put me in a position to smash the tyranny of the white man for ever." He grinned disarmingly. "You realise, of course, that when I say 'white man' I do recognise that there are some of you who are clean. You, Theodor—after the victory—will still be at my side."

"I understand entirely, Mr. President, and I am very grateful."

"Yes, this is a conference which will start the release of all my black brothers. It will pave their way to freedom from the yoke of oppression."

He was in a buoyant and confidential mood. "Yes, my friend Theodor, it is the most important conference and it will change the course of history."

"I have taken the precaution, Mr. President, of sending four of my most reliable men on ahead to vet security arrangements there."

Amin was instantly on the alert. "They will be discreet, I hope. My journey is a secret and it must stay a secret. Not until afterwards—a week afterwards, if it all goes as I intend—will it be announced. And that will be at the moment when I declare war."

"My men understand that perfectly, Mr. President. They are good men who can be trusted. They will be discreet." He rose to his feet. "Now Mr. President, if you will excuse me sir. I have duties to perform."

"What duties?"

"On an occasion as important as this one, sir, I feel it is essential that I search the aircraft personally."

"For bombs?"

"For anything, Mr. President. And, once I have searched it, I will have an armed guard mounted on it. No-one will be allowed near it, let alone into it, until we go on board tomorrow evening."

"When you have completed your work you will return to join me in a drink," said Amin. "We will drink to the successful outcome of this historic journey to Pemba."

"Thank you, Mr. President," said Theodor humbly. "It will be a great pleasure for me to drink to that."

Theodor, before summoning his soldiers, drove quickly to the Metropolitan where Barbra was waiting.

"All done?" he asked.

She nodded. "All done."

He suddenly realised she was smoking a cigarette. He had never seen her do so before. He indicated it. "That's unusual, isn't it, for you?"

"I always used to," she said. "I used to smoke many but my brother kept saying they were bad for one."

"And why now?"

She inhaled deeply and held the smoke for a few moments. Then, pursing her lips, she released it in three near-perfect rings. She watched with an almost childish pride as they drifted towards the high ceiling, buckling and distorting as they went. "I now think that perhaps the snuff is not . . . well . . . ladylike," she said. "It is not a good habit."

"Maybe," he said. "I've never fancied it myself." He discreetly handed her an envelope. "The Lefarge passport."

She slipped it into her handbag. Her eyes were clouded with anxiety. "You will be all right, won't you, Karl? This man . . . he won't hurt you too much."

"No more than he needs to." He glanced at his watch. "It's time I was away."

"Going to check on my work?" She was trying to keep her tone light.

"Something of that sort."

"Goodbye, Karl dear—and good luck." She turned abruptly and left him before he could respond.

Ten armed soldiers went with Theodor to the Citation jet—two officers, one sergeant and seven rankers. They reached the entrance. "Stay here," he instructed. "I'll do the search myself." They waited in the hangar.

He spent forty minutes in the plane, checking on Barbra's work and checking that no-one else could spot Barbra's work. Then he locked the door before climbing down to talk to the senior officer.

"Quite clean," he said. "Now . . . no-one is to enter that aircraft until the President and his party arrive tomorrow. That includes you and your men."

"Yes, sir."

"There's to be a permanent guard of six men, two in here and four outside the hangar. And I want them alert, so change the guard every two hours.

"And make certain they understand my orders. They're to shoot any unauthorised person who comes near this aircraft. Understand? They're to shoot and we'll worry about the questions afterwards."

"I understand, sir."

"Then carry on."

The other officer and one of the rankers escorted Theodor back to the Palace.

Amin, drinking with a select group of his senior men, greeted him effusively. "Ah, Theodor! What do you wish to drink? Beer . . . whisky . . . brandy?" Then, remembering, he added good-naturedly: "But, of course, you do not enjoy alcohol, do you? Well, there is still plenty of choice. Orange . . . lemon . . . tomato even . . ." He waved towards the huge side-board where the drinks were on display. "Just help yourself."

Theodor thanked him and went to the sideboard. There were three opened bottles of whisky and, for the first time in years, he felt tempted. He started to reach for the nearest one but, feeling guilty, he hesitated. He had a quick mental picture of his dead wife Sybille. And he wondered illogically if—wherever she was— she would really mind now, if she would still reproach him. Then he thought of what lay ahead of him, of the unknown man who would be waiting in the shadows of a lonely street. He was frightened by the prospect of the knife. He needed the courage, and yet . . .

He picked up the bottle and, still feeling curiously disloyal, he poured the whisky into his glass. It was a more-than-full measure, undiluted by ice or water.

"Why! That is good, that is very good," said Amin when he noticed. "Tonight you are drinking a man's drink, eh?"

"Tonight, Mr. President, is a special night."

"Of course it is," agreed Amin. He raised his glass. "To tomorrow and success!"

Theodor repeated the toast in a flat and solemn voice. The whisky was raw and burning as it coursed down his throat. He drained the glass and refilled it.

"I must take a walk," he said later. "The fresh air . . . it will clear my head."

And they joked about him after he had gone. He wasn't used to drink, that one. He was a tomato-juice man.

Theodor walked for twenty minutes after leaving the Palace. He turned off the main thoroughfare into a road that was narrower and darker. At the end of that road, well beyond the last of the buildings, he turned left into a deserted lane.

There were isolated mounds of bushes ahead of him on either side and he knew that behind one of them the man would be waiting. He did not know which mound it would be. Now that it was so near he was wondering if there could not have been an easier way. If the knife were to come too hard or too low . . .

He walked on unhurriedly, his boots harsh against the broken-stone surface and his body sticky with the sweat of apprehension. Something rustled in the bushes he was passing and he immediately tensed, waiting for the onslaught and the pain. There was nothing. It was a rat, perhaps, or a disturbed and fidgeting bird.

A lazy moon was watching him jaundicedly. A bat swooped low and the night was alive with the brittle raspings of the crickets.

He relaxed a little and again he moved on.

Now the moon was skulking behind a veil of cloud and, in the extra darkness, he felt still more vulnerable. He did not see the sinewy young man who moved so fast and so silently from his leafy hiding-place. He was not aware of him until the moment when the knife struck home.

*　　*　　*

Pierre Rey was about to drive to the aircraft when Barbra intercepted him outside his bungalow on Mengo Hill. "Here's the Lefarge passport," she said.

"What's this, then? I'm suppose to get that on the plane. That's what was agreed. Theodor—or whatever his name is—is supposed to give it to me on the plane."

"You haven't heard, then?"

He was still in his car, leaning towards her from the window. "Heard what?"

"About Theodor. About the attack."

He frowned, got out of the car, and slammed the door. "Look, if this is some sort of trick . . ."

She shook her head emphatically and he could see that she was genuinely upset. "He's dying. That's what the doctors say. He may even be dead by now."

"But what the hell's happened?"

"You remember that last attempt on his life—the one when Lajeba got killed. Well, they've tried again." Her lips were quivering and she was near to tears. "And this time they've got him. An old woman found him early today in a lane near the Palace. He was unconscious and in a terrible state, really terrible. He'd been knifed and kicked and . . . oh, it's too awful what they did to him . . ."

"Where is he?"

"The hospital."

"So he won't be on the flight."

"I told you," she said angrily. "They think he's dying."

"In that case it's off," he said flatly. "The whole thing—it's off. I'm not going through this lot, not on my own."

"You can't back down now. It's too late."

"I can and I will. That jet of mine is going to develop a mysterious engine fault. It's going to be unserviceable. And by the time I've got it fixed all that muck of yours will be out of it."

"You're talking like a fool."

"A fool, eh? I would be a fool, wouldn't I, if I went up there with that load of gas and without your friend. It's a trick."

"Phone the hospital and check for yourself."

He spat at the ground. "That wouldn't tell me anything. Hospitals can be fixed and I'm not flying, not with that plane as it is."

Suddenly she was composed and her voice was harsh. "Perhaps I should tell you that arrangements have already been made for your brother and his wife to be executed forty-eight hours from now. Their deaths will be automatic, unless the people holding them learn of the accident and of Idi Amin's death."

"Then you've got me trapped, haven't you? You've damn-well got me trapped."

"There's a big cash bait on the other side of the trap," she replied. "By this time tomorrow you could be on your way to a fortune and a new life."

He saw the flaw immediately. "How will I get the money now? Without Theodor I won't know where to go."

"There'll be a man in the aircraft that will be waiting for you. He'll know what to do and where to go. It was he who was going to take you to Switzerland, anyway. Not Theodor."

"And you really think he's going to die? Theodor, I mean."

"That's what they say at the hospital."

"Well, he was a slimy bastard. He had it coming."

Barbra flinched at his words but did not pick him up on them. "You realise exactly what this means, don't you?" she said. "The operation goes ahead exactly as planned. Only now you'll be the only one to escape alive out of the aeroplane. You've got your mask?"

"It's in the car."

"Theodor's place will probably be taken by a man called Ojok."

"I know Ojok. Well, I've seen him. He took over Lajeba's job when Lajeba caught it."

"Obviously he'll die with the others."

"Obviously." Pierre climbed back into the car. "This bleeper thing I've got—you quite sure it's powerful enough to do the job?"

"It can be picked up more than thirty miles away by somebody tuned into the right frequency."

"Well, I hope they're not thirty miles away. I don't like the water."

He started the engine. "See you sometime."

She nodded. "Good luck . . . Monsieur Lefarge."

*　　*　　*

The Citation jet was designed to carry eight people, including a crew of two. Amin's had been expensively adapted to give him more space and luxury. Just in front of the toilet compartment at the rear, where two standard forward-facing seats would normally have been secured, was a hugely-padded armchair. That was for the President.

Amin's two top advisors, the Minister of Foreign Affairs and the Minister of War, had the single seats facing him in the centre of the cabin, one to port and the other to starboard. At the front, immediately behind the flight-deck, was a specially-installed cocktail cabinet.

Ojok was seated next to Pierre Rey. Amin saw no need for a second crew member. He knew he had a fine and experienced man at the controls. He knew that the plane's automatic-pilot system was superb. And anyway—should there be any emergency—the Minister of War knew enough about flying to handle the plane.

They had all arrived at the airfield and embarked with the minimum of fuss.

Pierre went methodically through his pre-flight checks and, the moment he indicated his readiness, he was given clearance by Air Traffic Control. The plane surged along the runway and lifted smoothly into the approaching dusk.

Barbra spotted it as it passed over Kampala and she made a telephone call to a man in Nairobi. "Father's gone swimming," she said. Then she hung up.

The man in Nairobi asked for a number in Chicago, Illinois. And, when it came through, he was brief. "Father's gone swimming," he said.

"Thank you," said Stanton. He replaced the receiver. "Well, Hugo," he said to Dr. Engelman. "Let's have a drink. It's over."

*   *   *

One of Cherif's cousins had driven Weaver to the town of Tetuan. Now Weaver was in a bedroom at a cheap and fourth-rate hotel near the Sidi es Saidi mosque.

He was waiting for the call he had booked to Stanton. This was a pre-arranged call. He had been instructed to make it at precisely this time, during that briefing off the Isle of Wight.

He checked his watch with the wall clock and frowned with impatience. This was taking longer than he had expected.

The bell rang. "America is on the line," announced a man proudly. He made it sound like a State proclamation.

"Weaver?"

"Yes . . . how are you?"

His pleasantry was ignored. "Father's gone swimming."

"Hey! Hold it!" shouted Weaver urgently. He didn't want Stanton to hang up immediately.

"What is it?" Stanton sounded annoyed.

"I've got problems."

"Like what?"

"The girl—she knows Carter's identity."

"I see. Then handle it."

"In what way?"

"You're in charge in Morocco," said Stanton briskly. "Just handle it."

"Okay, okay. But how do you want me to handle it?"

"Think back," came the reply. "Remember the Dandenongs."

Then Weaver heard the click of the receiver going down in distant America. He settled his account and hurried to the truck. "Back to the caves," he said to Cherif's cousin. "There's a job to be done."

* * *

The English doctor with the narrow head was fussing short-sightedly along the hospital corridors when he was stopped by a black medical orderly.

"Well?" he asked querulously. "What is it?"

"Dr. Obothi heard you were here sir," said the orderly. "He told me to ask if you could spare him a few minutes."

"Why?"

"He has a white patient sir. A German. And he would like your opinion."

"Germans are not my affair," grumbled the English doctor. "I have too much to do without bothering about Germans."

He was in the hospital, in fact, merely to make a courtesy call on a High Commissioner's wife who had undergone an operation for piles. Now he was looking forward to a few hands of bridge. "Not my affair at all," he repeated. "I'm not here for Germans."

"But this man is very important," persisted the orderly. "And Dr. Obothi is most anxious."

"Really, this is a gross impertinence." But he still followed the orderly along the corridor and allowed himself to be ushered into a side-room. "Is this the man?"

The question was hardly necessary. There was only one bed in the room. "Yes sir," said the orderly. "I'll fetch Dr. Obothi right away sir."

The doctor rubbed at his bald and narrow head. "Hmm . . . something peculiar here," he muttered. "I'm sure I've seen this fellow somewhere before."

*   *   *

Cherif and one of his cousins climbed to a boulder-screened spot high above the entrance to the caves and there they dug the grave. They dug it carefully and discreetly. Then, after hiding the spades, they reported to Weaver.

"Would you like me to see to it?" asked Cherif.

"No," said Weaver grimly. "This is one job I've got to do myself."

Yvette was asleep in the inner cave and Marcel, pale and dejected, was in the central one.

"Go and join your wife," said Weaver.

"Why should I?" Marcel's face was sulky, his voice was petulant.

"Because I'm damned well telling you to, that's why. Now get in there and stay there until I say you can come out."

"I don't know how much longer you're going to keep up this silly game," said Marcel. But he did as he was told.

Weaver gestured to Cherif and his cousins. They followed Marcel.

He braced himself and took a deep breath. Then, his features firm with resolution, he moved quietly to the outer cave and there he stopped. From the entrance he could see the hunched mound of Carter's back. Carter was on a low rock, smoking as usual.

"Most of them are married." That's what Carter had said. He'd said it in a sneering, almost patronising, sort of way.

The words had reminded Weaver of a long-past night in a place called Broken Hill. They had reminded him of a man called Sharp and a man called Porter. They had reminded him of the faithless wife he had once loved so dearly. And they had brought the sour bile of hatred into his throat.

He stood there for a moment or two, looking at Carter's back. There was that familiar tight feeling again in his chest as the old resentments and loathings began welling within him. Porter and Carter. They were so very similar . . .

Weaver made no sound as he crept up behind Carter. And suddenly his strong hands were around Carter's throat.

Carter gave a choked-off yelp of startled surprise. His arms and legs jerked stiffly in a convulsive reflex. Then he began clawing at Weaver's fingers. He was trying, with the despair of desperation, to prize them away.

Weaver squeezed tighter, the muscles of his own neck prominent and rigid with effort. He was surprised that Carter, a powerful man, put up such a puny fight.

He laid the body beside the rock and went to the inner cave to fetch Cherif. The cousins stayed with the prisoners.

It was a struggle for them to carry Carter up the steep incline to the grave. They dropped him in and, working quickly and methodically, they covered him with five feet of earth and stones.

Weaver was sweating as, eventually, he rested his spade. "Well, this time I got the right bastard," he said.

"What does that mean?" asked Cherif.

"Forget it," replied Weaver. "It's an old, old story."

They hid the spades again for Cherif to dispose of later. "Time the transport was here," said Weaver. He had hardly spoken before they could hear the engine of the truck struggling up towards them. "Come on—let's get loaded and get the hell out of here."

The covered truck, with false number plates, was travelling without lights. By the time it reached its destination, within walking distance of the caves, they were ready.

"Now where are you taking us?" demanded Marcel.

"Cut the questions," said Weaver. "Get in the truck." He took Yvette's elbow and pushed her forward. "You too."

Weaver and two of Cherif's cousins travelled with them in the back. It was impossible for them to know where they were going or, indeed, where they had been.

The driver aimed for Ouezzane and then took the left fork on to the main highway towards Fez.

"Here's money," said Weaver. "Enough to get you out of trouble." He handed it to Marcel. "Your passports will be put in the post." He gave them the name of a hotel in Casablanca. "Go there and ask for them."

"Why can't you just give them to us?" demanded Yvette.

"Because I do the deciding, that's why. And, incidentally, there'll be no point in asking the concierge why he's got the passports. He won't know. Neither will anybody else there."

"But we must have our passports," protested Marcel. "How can we identify ourselves without them?"

"You're a travelling man," said Weaver. "You'll cope."

"Where is Dickie?" said Yvette suddenly. "I didn't see him when we left the caves."

"Mr. Richards, you mean?"

"You know exactly who I mean."

In the gloom of the truck they could not see the way Weaver's left eye was twitching. "He was called away," he said. "Rather unexpectedly."

Now they were obviously off the road for the truck was bumping and pitching over rugged terrain. Then it stopped. "Right—everybody out," said Weaver. "This is the end of the line."

He climbed down into the desert night and the Reys followed him. The two Moroccans stayed in the truck.

"I suggest you walk that way." Weaver was pointing to the south. "There's a village. You should make it in about two hours."

He swung back up into the truck and it started to pull away.

"Please—you can't leave us here—not like this!" shouted Marcel.

"And don't worry about your Turkish stuff," called Weaver. "You'll get it okay. That's a promise."

Then he was gone. They were never to see him again.

*   *   *

Somewhere down there in the darkness, about 25,000 feet below them, was the edge of the Indian Ocean. This, Pierre Rey knew, was the moment. He was trembling, just slightly, with nervousness and his mouth felt dry as a sun-bleached bone.

Ojok, he reassured himself, knew nothing of the technicalities of the flight-deck. Aeroplane flight, to him, was just a baffling miracle and he would give no cause for worry.

Pierre checked his altitude and his speed. Then, satisfied, he relinquished control to the autopilot.

Ojok, his great flap of a top lip hanging down loosely over the lower one, was still staring bovinely into the murk beyond the bird-proof windscreen. He was lost in his own thoughts. Or perhaps in no thoughts at all.

Pierre felt under his seat to reassure himself. The mask was still there, of course, just as he had known it would be . . . but feeling its nearness made him feel somehow safer.

To the right of the control panel was a switch which the manufacturers had not installed. Pierre's finger hesitated over it for two tremulous seconds and then, determinedly, he pressed it down.

The emergency oxygen masks in the cabin did not drop down but, from their vents, the deadly nerve-gas began seeping. It did not hiss. It did not make any sound at all. It just seeped silently and insidiously. And it had no odour.

Pierre knew that the concentration of gas would build up more quickly in the cabin than on the flight-deck and he needed to get Ojok out of the way . . . so that he could clamp on his mask.

He glanced over his shoulder, peering through the partly-opened folding partition. Amin was sleeping peacefully in the giant armchair, his head slumped against his chest. It seemed to Pierre that the other men—the Minister of Foreign Affairs and the Minister of War—were also asleep. The backs of their heads were so very still and that of the Minister of War was uncomfortably pillowed against the starboard body of the plane.

"Quick, Ojok!" said Pierre. "The President is sick. See to him."

Ojok panicked out of his reverie and was instantly on his feet, stumbling clumsily through the partition in his anxiety.

Pierre snatched for his mask.

Amin was startled awake by Ojok's sudden entrance. He looked at him with distaste. "Yes? What is it?"

"Mr. President sir . . . I thought . . . that is, we thought . . ."

Ojok seemed to be having difficulty in forming his words. He lurched forward a few drunken paces and then stood there swaying, his eyes wide like those of a hurt and bewildered animal.

"What did you think?" snapped Amin.

Ojok gasped and made disgusting, unintelligible noises as he tried to reply. He clutched at his throat and his knees began to buckle. Then, in grotesque slow-motion, he crumpled to the carpet.

Amin tried to lever himself up to go to him but his arms were unaccountably leaden. They would not respond to the instructions from his brain. His legs were also paralysed and he could see by their immobility—and by their fixed expressions of terror—that his two ministers were afflicted in exactly the same way. And still the gas went on pouring into the plane.

Pierre, now safe in his tested mask, double-checked that he had his bleeper. That was his link with the boats down there waiting, the boats which would carry him to safety. Soon he would be on the flight to Switzerland and the money . . .

He turned on the tape-recorder and his transmitter. His disembodied voice was harshly metallic but calm and professional: "This is Uncle George Apple . . . Oner Zero Oner . . . Uncle George Apple, Oner Zero Oner . . . do you read me? Over . . . do you read me please?"

Pierre glimpsed the live but transfixed bodies behind him. He saw the amazement and the horror in Amin's eyes. And he was glad he had tested the mask.

"Mayday . . . Mayday . . . this is Uncle George Apple, Oner Zero One . . . Mayday . . ." Now there was more urgency in the mechanical message. Just a suggestion of panic.

He started to reach for the black parachute which was stowed under the co-pilot's seat. Suddenly his arms went limp and he flopped, flaccid as wet bread, towards the glowing lights of the controls.

"Mayday . . . Mayday . . ." said his recorded voice. "Come in, please . . . my controls have jammed . . ."

*   *   *

Barbra lit another cigarette. She sipped her gin and reflected, not without satisfaction, on the savage twist in the scheme.

Theodor, she knew, had omitted to tell Pierre Rey one small fact about the XV range of gases. They tended to condense easily into moisture and, in that form, they penetrated the pores of the skin.

Stanton had explained it all so clearly during that meeting on the boat off Cowes. And, to emphasize the accuracy of his information, he had quoted a statement made in 1975 by Brigadier-General Rothschild, who was once director of chemical, biological and radiological warfare with the United States Army Chemical Corps:

One tiny absorbed droplet—which might not even be noticed for it caused no pain—was enough to cause death.

Barbra stubbed the cigarette and glanced at her watch. It should be happening, she thought, just about this time. And she wondered, with an almost clinical detachment, about what was going on aboard that aircraft.

This particular variation of the gas, she knew, was singularly fast and efficient. It robbed a man, almost immediately, of his voice and his powers of movement. However, it took far longer to attack his lungs, heart and brain—particularly if he had the protection of a mask.

So Pierre Rey would be able to breathe and think. He would still be aware of what was happening around him. But he would be able to do nothing about it . . .

*   *   *

Terror, writhing like a fistful of spade-mutilated worms, was filling his stomach. And Pierre Rey, now realising how he had been deceived, knew that death was near. But, even in his helpless desperation, he tried to smother the thought. He was a fighter, one of nature's survivors, and while he could still think there remained just the glimmer of hope. He clung to that glimmer, struggling in his mind for some means of salvation.

And still his voice went on beseeching from the tape: "Uncle George Apple, Oner Zero Oner . . . I have the President of Uganda aboard and I need help . . . come in, somebody, please . . . my controls are jammed . . ."

*   *   *

"Really, Obothi, this is too bad, it really is too bad," grumbled the English doctor. "Now I've completely missed my bridge and for such trivialities."

"But doctor, I—"

"Don't 'but doctor' me, man. Wasting my time like that. There's nothing serious there, nothing serious at all. A child of three could have told you that."

"Yes, but—"

"A few bruises on the face—eh? A few bruises and a broken cheek-bone. You have seen a broken cheek-bone before, I suppose?"

"Yes, of course, doctor."

"A superficial knife wound in the shoulder. Nothing to worry about there, is there?"

"And the leg, of course."

"What exactly do you mean by 'of course'? I saw the leg, didn't I? I examined it. It's fractured, that's all. Fractured in two places."

"That's exactly what I wanted to ask you about, doctor. That leg. Do you think it will leave him with a limp?"

"A *limp*?" He stressed the word to emphasise his disgust and he looked sternly at the black man as if suspecting him of having emitted a nasty smell. "How can I tell? Perhaps it will, perhaps it won't. I wouldn't have thought so myself, but who's to say?

"Anyway, he's a German and Germans aren't my responsibility."

And the English doctor stalked off angrily to his car.

*　　*　　*

The distress messages from the Citation jet were being heard at receiving stations as far apart as Mombasa, Zanzibar and Dar-es-Salaam. They were also being picked up by shipping.

Emergency services were alerted and radar teams tried, in vain, to get a location fix on the mystery plane.

Many radio operators were trying to reply but, it seemed to them, the plane's radio had developed a fault. It could transmit but not receive.

Politicians and officials, summoned for advice, were perplexed by the repeated references to the President of Uganda. How could he possibly be up there in that plane? He couldn't even be in the area, for they would have been warned in advance.

There was now unmistakable fear in the voice reaching them from the black, cloud-banked heights. "Mayday . . . Mayday . . . can anybody hear me . . . please come in somebody . . ."

They tried and they went on trying. Still the voice pleaded to be heard. And Pierre Rey was inert and helpless on the flight-deck—listening to himself describing his fate.

"This is Uncle George Apple, Oner Zero Oner . . . for God's sake, please . . . please . . . I can't shift my controls . . . my controls are locked . . . can anybody hear me . . .?"

In his agitation, before turning on the gas, he had

forgotten the advice Barbra had given him at the bungalow. "I suggest you start jettisoning the fuel immediately after you've switched on the gas." That's what she had said. But he had forgotten.

There was a brief whirring noise as the tape reached the end of the reel, and then the listeners below could hear no more.

The aircraft, they concluded, had obviously crashed and, as near as they could work it out, it was about two hundred miles from land.

Helicopters with powerful searchlights were scrambled into the air. Lifeboats were launched and shipping was ordered to converge on the area.

Still the jet, with fuel for another five hundred miles, continued through the night skies at a constant speed of 340 knots.

Only Pierre was still alive. Amin and the others in the cabin had died before the ending of the tape.

So, still conscious and aware, he flew on through the darkness with his cargo of four dead men. He could hear the smoothly changing tones of the engines, the mindlessly-efficient clickings of the autopilot, and even the frightened beating of his own heart. He could hear all these things but he could do nothing. And now even his breathing was becoming laboured.

There were splutterings as the engines sought to suck up the last of the fuel. They coughed and choked and finally they died. And Pierre was still alive as the plane began its long and graceful glide downwards.

It fell faster as it lost speed. There was nothing graceful about it now. It wasn't gliding, not any more. It was dropping out of the sky. Just spinning and tumbling in an orgasm of destruction.

The bodies in the cabin, Amin's on top of the others, were battered against the flight-deck partition as they smashed into the water. The belly of the jet was split wide open.

Then a wave enveloped them and they were sucked down to the depths.

* * *

There was dandruff, like flakes of hoar-frost, on the shoulders of his once-smart grey suit. His tired face was wizened, more because of years of drinking than merely because of the years. Now he had emptied a glass or so too many and he was bored with his own company. "Funny, isn't it?" he said. "Funny how things work out."

Stanton, drinking alone, resented the intrusion. There was no-one else near, so the words were obviously being aimed at him. He stared straight ahead, watching the man in the mirror behind the bar. "What things?"

"This Amin business." The man indicated the main story on the front page of his newspaper. "Going like that. Bloody ironic, isn't it . . ."

Stanton grunted disinterestedly.

"Don't you think so?" demanded the man.

"Yes, I suppose so . . ."

"No *suppose* about it," said the man indignantly. "It bloody is—no two ways about it." He leaned forward confidentially. "You just think of the people who've tried to kill that bastard. Dozens of 'em, there've been." He rubbed the side of his nose with pantomime significance as if he was allowing Stanton into an important secret. "Absolutely bloody dozens of 'em. Then what does the joker go and do? He goes and gets himself knocked off in an accident."

He thumped the newspaper in disgust as if he was angry that Amin, by the style of his death, had been guilty of some final and unforgivable impertinence. "Typical of the bastard," he said bitterly. "But, still, you can't say it's not ironic."

"No," said Stanton flatly. "I can't say that."

'Not that it'll make any difference," said the man.

"You mark my words, mister. It won't make any difference at all. Some other nut will take his place . . ."

Stanton drained his drink and walked out into the Chicago night. It was starting to drizzle and he pulled up the collar of his coat. Yes, he thought, that was a disturbing possibility. Perhaps some man even more dangerous than Amin could now seize power in Uganda . . .

"Oh, what the hell . . . that's not my concern," he said to himself. "I had a job to do and I've done it."

But the doubt would not go away. It stayed there, festering malignantly at the back of his mind . . .

EPILOGUE

Cherif did buy his store in Tangier. In fact, together with his cousins, he did far better than he had ever anticipated. Soon they were owning six stores and the leather-goods factory which kept them supplied. And Cherif always smoked English cigarettes because, as he was constantly explaining, they were his *best* favourites . . .

Weaver never returned to Australia. The Dandenong mountains and the city of Melbourne held too many painful memories. So, for that matter, did the whole country. He bought himself a ranch in California and arranged for his daughter Karen to join him. And he tried to forget the days of violence . . .

Barbra exchanged regular letters with Theodor when she returned to Poland after her tour in Uganda. Then she managed to get a visa for a holiday abroad, for a sentimental journey back to Coblenz. The beautiful old Rhine-side home of her girlhood, once cherished by the Rademachers, had been turned into a small private hotel. And it was there that, once again, she had met Theodor. After the first day or two she hardly noticed the limp which he was to have for the rest of his life.

"Come back with me," he had said impulsively one evening. "Come back with me to Munich. We could get married."

She had shaken her head. "Karl, my dear, I don't really think I'm the marrying sort," she had said quietly. "But I will come with you, just for a while, to Munich . . ."

*   *   *

Soon the removal men would be arriving to strip the rented office in Chicago. A man called Durrant sat thoughtfully behind the huge glass-topped desk, savouring it all for the last time. He was a chubby man with protruding bulbous eyes. Some people thought he looked rather like a paunchy bullfrog.

Most of his files had already been destroyed. Now, from the top right-hand drawer of the desk, he took a sheaf of neatly-typed documents and an American passport bearing the name "Stanton."

On the table in a corner of the office was a small mechanical shredder. He fed the documents and the passport into it and soon paper was spiralling out in thin strips which looked like spaghetti.

Durrant ripped up the strips and took them to the washroom adjoining the office. And there he flushed them down the lavatory.

He had to pull the chain three times before the last pieces finally disappeared down towards the Chicago sewers. And then, at last, Stanton was dead.

Except, of course, that there had never really been a man called Stanton.

AVON/31617/$1.95

SLOWLY, AT FIRST,
THEN WITH SHUDDERING
HORROR...YOU EXPERIENCE
THE ULTIMATE
ACT OF TERRORISM!

THE VIKING PROCESS

NORMAN HARTLEY

"Does for terrorism what Frederick Forsyth did for assassination in THE DAY OF THE JACKAL and John Le Carre did for espionage in THE SPY WHO CAME IN FROM THE COLD. . . . There is no let up on the pace until the very last moment!"
BOSTON HERALD AMERICAN

SELECTED BY BOOK-OF-THE-MONTH CLUB AND PLAYBOY BOOK CLUB

VIKE 2-77